THE **MESSENGER** AND THE **MALADIC TRANSFER**

*"A life is not important except
in the impact it has on other lives."*
EPITAPH ON JACKIE ROBINSON'S TOMBSTONE

Michael K. Parson

Author of
*The Inheritance: A Story of Love, Legacy,
and Lost Opportunities*

Book and cover design by Daniel Ruesch Design

Alpine, Utah | www.danielruesch.net

ISBN 979-8-218-54113-2

WHAT READERS ARE SAYING:

"In Michael K. Parson's *The Messenger and The Maladic Transfer*, he tells a tale of love, loss, and longing. But on a deeper level it is a narrative of life's lessons learned through experiencing that love, loss, and longing that transforms the soul. Here is a book that inspires us to be better people. One cannot help but reflect on their own life's purpose, meaning, and contributions to others as they read this powerful story. It's the kind of story that you keep going back to mentally over and over, long after you've finished reading it — it's that engaging and reflective. You will never look at others — and yourself — the same way again after reading *The Messenger and The Maladic Transfer*."

— KYLE N. WEIR, PH.D., LMFT
  Marriage and Family Therapist
  Professor – Counselor Education Program
  California State University – Fresno

"I was so touched by this story; it brought tears to my eyes and felt the spirit of it. It is so well written and easy to read, I couldn't put it down. It left me pondering on the meaning of my life, am I learning the lessons I am supposed to through my experiences and trials? Am I growing to my spiritual potential? It certainly opens my eyes and heart to others more; and hope that I can fulfill my mission in life by serving more."

— JANINA COBAR, Author of *My Prayers, His Miracles*

"*The Messenger and the Maladic Transfer* by Michael K. Parson is not just a novel; it's an emotional and spiritual journey that leaves an indelible mark on your heart. From the very first page, Nathan Reynolds' story grips you, blending the weight of real-world tragedy with a mystical, soul-stirring moral dilemma. Parson beautifully captures the struggles of being human—the fear of mortality, the search for redemption, and the longing for purpose.

What makes this book truly special is how it not only entertains but also prompts deep reflection. As Nathan faces an unimaginable choice—whether to transfer his terminal illness to someone else—the reader is invited to ponder their own beliefs about sacrifice, morality, and the meaning of life. This isn't just about the dilemma of one man, but about the choices we all face in the darkest moments of our lives.

The novel's exploration of love, resilience, and spiritual growth is both heartfelt and profound. It pushes us to consider our capacity for empathy and strength, even in our most difficult times. Parson's storytelling will make you pause, reflect, and appreciate the connections you have with others.

More than just a book, *The Messenger and the Maladic Transfer* is an experience—one that will stay with you long after the final page. A must-read for anyone seeking not only entertainment but a deeper understanding of the human spirit.
—PAUL FINLAYSON
   Principal, Alpine School District

"This novel touched my heart in ways I didn't expect. It's a beautiful and profound exploration of what it means to be human, to face life's toughest challenges, and to search for meaning in the face of uncertainty. From the first page, the story pulls you in, not just with its captivating plot, but with its emotional depth and the way it speaks to the soul.

"The author has an incredible gift for portraying the struggles we all face — the moments of doubt, the fear of the unknown, and the longing for hope and redemption. Through the journey of the characters, I found myself reflecting on my own life, on the choices I've made, and the challenges I've overcome. It's rare for a book to not only entertain but to offer such deep insights into the human spirit.

"What moved me the most was the way the novel explores themes of love, resilience, and the search for purpose. It reminds us that even in our darkest moments, we have the capacity to grow, to find strength, and to connect with others in meaningful ways. The writing is heartfelt and honest, filled with moments that will make you pause and reflect on your own path.

"This is more than just a story, it's an emotional experience that will stay with you long after you've finished reading. It's the kind of book that makes you want to hug your loved ones a little tighter and approach life with a deeper sense of gratitude and compassion.

"I highly recommend this novel to anyone who seeks a story that not only entertains but also uplifts, inspires, and challenges you to think about what truly matters in life."
— MARJORIE ROMAN

"Such a sweet, powerful story! It is a captivating read that will keep you enthralled to the end, and is filled with life lessons. Definitely a book that is and will be treasured by many!!"
— NATALIE DEIM

"Michael K. Parson is an incredible writer. I get engrossed in the story! It develops in a very fascinating way so you can't stop reading! As the story resolves, a warm comfortable feeling comes over you."
— DEBORAH ROMNEY

"How does one become insightful?— By living through a variety of thought provoking, soul searching, and even spiritually trying experiences of their own. This is an observation derived from having known Michael K. Parson for, at this point in our mortal existence, over fifty years. He uses his own life experiences to creatively include his readers in beautifully written, carefully throughout, insightful stories of life, death, and beyond. This story stirs the soul and intellect by ushering one through a full range of emotions which terminate on a spiritual high. A peek through this story portal into the life of the main character, Nathaniel Reynolds, will bring relatable insight into your life as well."
— ETHELYN BRADSHAW

"The dichotomies in this story made me think. It's a story of the pain resulting from poorly made decisions and the elation of choosing the right — opportunities lost versus reaching for a legacy of goodness — and the overwhelming power of the temptation to put our own desires first, regardless of the cost to others, versus reaching up and grasping the higher self.

"Michael K. Parson delivers a charmingly retro tale, set in a time when roles were more defined and the lines between right and wrong were a little more clear, but not neccessarily easier to choose. It's a pleasant and thought-provoking read."
— DANIEL RUESCH
    President, Daniel Ruesch Design | Book Designer

TO MY INCREDIBLE WIFE, TERRY—
your unwavering love, patience, and belief in me
have carried me through once again. Your faith,
especially during the moments I doubted myself, has
been a guiding light. As always, your encouragement
and countless hours as my trusted copy editor have
made this book possible. I am endlessly grateful
for your partnership in this journey. Terry, I love
you more than words can express. Thank you for
standing by me, for believing in me, and for making
my dreams a reality—again.

Disclaimer

All of the characters in this story are fictitious, only figments of my imagination. Any resemblance to any of my relatives, friends, associates, or acquaintances is purely coincidental. So, even if you think the shoe fits, don't wear it!

Acknowledgements

My thanks to Traci Parson, Ben Parson, Natalie Deim, Rachael Chappell, Marion Edwards, Cortney Finlayson, Marjorie Roman, Daniel Ruesch and many other friends and relatives, for their invaluable help in reading, proofreading, editing, and offering numerous suggestions as well as encouragement. I am grateful.

IT WAS SOME TIME BEFORE he began to sense that he was no longer alone in the room. Fear began to overtake him as he looked to his left, then to his right, but the room was so dark he could only see shadowy images. The feeling of someone else nearby was so strong that he slowly and hesitantly reached for the lamp on the nightstand. He could feel his heart pounding in his chest and instantly thought of Edgar Allan Poe's story, *The Tell-Tale Heart.* In those few seconds before his fingers reached the lamp, he thought of every horror story or movie he had ever read, seen, or heard of. As he touched the lamp, he could feel a cold sweat over much of his body. His hands felt especially clammy as his fingers slipped around the lamp and he fumbled with the switch.

◨ ◨ ◨

As light flooded the room, he felt a sense of relief as he could now see clearly. He quickly scanned the entire room to identify the person he sensed was there. His eyes looked back and forth, up and down, but he saw no one and began to feel a bit calmer. Yet, still fearing that someone really was in his room, he called out, "Who's there?" while clutching the baseball bat he kept under his bed for security. He still heard nothing but could not shake the feeling that he was not alone. Raising his voice, he again demanded, "Who's there?"

Suddenly, he found it hard to believe what unfolded next....

Michael K. Parson

CHAPTER

1

Michael K. Parson

❑ ❑ ❑

HIS NAME IS NATHAN REYNOLDS. Nathan is short for Nathaniel, but he has always preferred the shorter nickname, since Nathaniel seemed too biblical for him. His grandfather suggested the name and wrote in his baby book, "I hope when you think about your name, you will think of Nathaniel of old and emulate the character of him who had no guile." Nathan was twelve years old before he even knew what the word "guile" meant.

His grandparents on his mother's side died before he was born, as had his father's mother. His father's father, Grandpa Reynolds, died when Nathan was only five years old, leaving him with but few memories of his grandfather. He could remember his grandpa taking him to the park and pushing him on the swing. Whenever he thought about the swinging experience, he remembered screaming, "Higher, Grandpa, higher!" He also had fond memories of being pushed by his grandfather on the merry-go-round. That always made him dizzy.

Nathan was raised as an only child in the Midwest town of Stillwater, Oklahoma, where he enjoyed growing up with his friends. He supposed that his childhood would be considered uneventful since he must have had the same kinds of experiences most young boys had who were raised in similar circumstances.

His father tried taking him fishing when he was little. He was told that if he learned to fish well, his dad would someday take him marlin fishing on the ocean. While at first he thought that sounded exciting, he quickly decided that it was too boring just sitting there waiting for the fish to take a bite, so he looked for more interesting things to do in the water. He preferred skipping rocks, which apparently scared the fish away, so he was never asked to go fishing again. His intent was not to scare away the fish but simply to keep himself entertained.

Many of his friends enjoyed playing baseball. He thought it was okay but had read somewhere that the game of baseball was "five minutes of action stretched into five hours." That seemed to him to be a perfect description of the game.

* * *

Before Nathan started school, he loved watching TV with his mom. She would fix lunch for them, and they would watch Perry Mason together. It was then that he secretly began dreaming of one day becoming a lawyer like Perry Mason—always solving the case by the end of the show.

Once school started, he missed their lunchtime courtroom dramas, but during vacation periods, it was the highlight of his day. He remembered wishing he could be sick enough to stay home from school and watch the show with his mom, but not so sick that he couldn't enjoy it.

He also watched the movie *To Kill a Mockingbird*, where Gregory Peck portrayed Atticus Finch, a country lawyer who defended his clients against all odds. He was really inspired by that story. In many ways, Atticus Finch influenced him even more than Perry Mason. Nathan was especially moved at the close of the courtroom scene when the entire balcony stood and waited for Atticus to gather up his things and start walking out of the room. They waited until he had left the room to show their profound respect for him. Nathan decided that he wanted to become the kind of lawyer who could earn that same kind of respect.

Nathan loved his parents and enjoyed them too. However, they were in their late forties when he was born, so the older he got, the greater the generation gap seemed to be. Despite the difference in their ages, he did not think there was any kind of a gap between him and his grandpa. He remembered they always had fun together. Maybe there was some truth to what his dad always told him. He had said, "You may not remember, but your grandpa always seemed to be going through his second childhood." When Nathan asked his dad what he meant, he was told, "Your grandpa never grew up. He would rather play with the kids than spend time with the grown-ups!"

As Nathan grew older, he realized it wasn't that his grandpa never grew up, it was more that he took the time to help Nathan learn from his experiences and grow from them, even though he often made mistakes.

* * *

During his first year of high school Nathan discovered that he really enjoyed running. While Nathan was only a freshman, the coach saw great potential in him and gave him lots of encouragement. He not only enjoyed it, but every boy that he ran against found that Nathan was exceptionally good at it, too. By his junior year he was the league champion in cross-country.

Nathan's senior year was his most exciting. He continued to improve through the year in both track and cross-country, and the local paper played up the rivalry between him and another boy from a nearby school, which only motivated Nathan more. When track season began in the spring, the rivalry for the state mile championship only got stronger. The paper's sportswriter reported, "The competition for the varsity mile run between these two track stars is heating up, folks! I think we can plan to see a new state mile record this year."

What Nathan hadn't planned on was what happened during the varsity final for the mile run. He later shared with the reporter, "We were on the fourth lap of the mile, and I was just beginning my 'kick' and felt confident I was going to win the race. I was taken by surprise by what occurred when I took the lead coming off the final turn. I was beginning to pull away from the competition when, for the first time in my competitive career, I took a fall in the middle of the track and ended up in third place. I was humiliated in front of the large crowd that had gathered for this championship event. When I was asked if I was all right, I checked my arms and legs, walked around in a circle, then ran a few yards and came back to report that 'Yes, I seem to be fine—other than a little humiliation!'"

"So, how did that make you feel after the expectation of winning?" the reporter asked him.

"I was especially bothered by the fact that I had bragged to all my friends of how I was going to win the state championship and set a new state record. Now I felt like I was somewhat of a laughingstock at school."

With Nathan's high school years coming to a close, he planned on continuing his running in college. But since the "fall" incident he wasn't sure that he wanted to anymore. It just seemed so unfair when he had worked so hard toward winning the race. It would take him a long time to accept the fact that life could be so unfair, no matter how hard you worked for something. He realized that he might still have many disappointments in the future, but at his age he had a very bright future to look forward to.

So as far as his future in running was concerned, he decided to wait until summer was over before making a final decision, since if it hadn't been for his stumble and fall, he would have been the state champion. He realized that he still had the ability and potential but thought it wise just to wait and see.

CHAPTER

2

□ □ □

"What lies behind you and what lies in front of you,
pales in comparison to what lies inside of you."
RALPH WALDO EMERSON

AFTER GRADUATING FROM HIGH SCHOOL, Nathan attended the local college. During his freshman year, he met and became quite infatuated with the cutest girl on campus. At least to him, she was the cutest girl at school. One of the things that most attracted him to her was the fact that she wore a small white daisy painted by her right eye. *Really cute*, he thought.

Her name was Natalie Bremmer. Her parents had named her after the Hollywood actress, Natalie Wood. Nathan wasn't quite sure why—he just assumed they must have really liked the actress. He thought she resembled the movie star, especially when her hair was fixed a certain way. She was really beautiful, Nathan believed, particularly because she would smile at him whenever he passed by.

When he finally got the courage to ask her out, he was disappointed to hear her say, "I'm sorry, but I'm busy that night." A few days later, he asked her to an activity on campus, and again she turned him down. He couldn't understand it because he thought they were becoming such good friends. Why did she keep turning him down? He decided that maybe she wasn't really interested, but he wanted to give her at least one more chance. So while they walked each other to their classes the following day, he asked her, "I wondered if you could check your social calendar for this Friday night. If you're not busy, would you like to go to a movie or something?"

She gave him a sad look and said, "I'm sorry, but I'm not available that night either."

He sort of laughed, or at least tried to, and said, "You didn't even check your calendar! Are you sure about that?"

She smiled and said, "Yes, I'm sure, but I appreciate you asking."

They walked along quietly for a minute, although it seemed like several minutes to Nathan. As they arrived at her classroom he said, "Well, I guess I'll see you later."

"Yes, I'll see you after class," Natalie responded.

Nathan smiled and waved, but as he turned to walk away, he felt very dejected. He wondered why she never said "yes."

* * *

Natalie entered her class and sat down next to Emily, her best friend. Emily asked her, "So how are things with you and Nathan?"

"It's a bit of a problem," she responded. "He keeps asking me out, but it's always on a night that I'm already busy."

"That's not a very big problem. Why don't *you* ask *him* out?" Emily suggested. Natalie just looked at her as Emily pointed to a poster on the wall advertising the Sadie Hawkins Day dance coming up on November 15th. "You know what that is, don't you?" When Natalie had a blank look on her face Emily added, "It's the annual girls' choice dance, and the boys aren't allowed to say no! At least that's supposed to be the rule."

Natalie had heard of Sadie Hawkins but had never been to one. She had understood that it was where girls ask the guys out, but that was the extent of her understanding.

"Yes, that's right," Emily responded. "It started in a Li'l Abner comic strip years ago. And the tradition is that the boy isn't supposed to refuse! At least you hope he won't refuse."

When Natalie caught up to Nathan after class, she grabbed his arm and said, "Can I ask you something?"

"Sure," he responded.

"Would you be willing to go with me to the Sadie Hawkins dance coming up on November 15?"

He thought, *WOW! Maybe she does like me! There may be hope after all.* He tried not to look too surprised when he said with a grin, "Yes, I'd love to. Thanks for asking me."

* * *

Sadie Hawkins Dance:

Soon after they arrived, they ran into Emily and her date, John. After visiting a bit, they heard the announcement, "For this next dance only, everyone should switch partners." Most of the students just looked at each other, not sure what to do. The announcer continued, "Come on, they won't bite. It will be fun! Please switch partners." Nathan and Natalie switched with Emily and John. As soon as they began dancing,

Nathan said to Emily, "I understand you may have had something to do with this evening?"

Emily laughed and responded, "Oh, what makes you think that?"

"Natalie told me how you suggested that she ask me to the dance."

"She did, did she?" Emily said, chuckling.

"Yes, and I want to thank you. I think you were inspired!" Nathan added.

Emily laughed again.

When the music was finished, everyone switched back to their original dates. Natalie said to Nathan, "Welcome back. Did you have fun?"

"Yes, I did, and I thanked her for suggesting that you invite me to the dance."

Natalie giggled.

* * *

After the dance, a group of them went to one of the most popular college hangouts in the country. Eskimo Joe's boasted to be Stillwater's "Jumpin Little Juke Joint!" It was voted "Best College Post-Game Hangout" by Sporting News and #3 in "The Perfect 10 of College Sports Bars" by Sports Illustrated! Eskimo Joe's claimed to be world famous for their cheese fries, which were a favorite of Nathan's. Another of his Eskimo Joe's favorite dishes was "Tootie's Buttermilk Pie."

* * *

After they had been on a few dates together, Nathan asked her, "So Natalie, if you were actually interested in me, why did you turn me down those three times?" Before she could answer, he confessed, "Because I had pretty much decided that after the third turn down, I wasn't going to ask you again. I was afraid that maybe you just weren't interested!"

Natalie chuckled. "First of all, I truly was busy on those nights you had asked me. But I really was interested, and I could tell that you were discouraged and might not ask again. So, I figured the best way to keep you interested was for me to ask you out." They both laughed. "Fortunately, the Sadie Hawkins Dance was coming up. That made it perfect for me to ask you!"

With a huge grin, Nathan responded, "Thank heavens for Sadie Hawkins Day!" Nathan knew now to ask her way in advance, and if she was busy, he was smart enough to keep asking until he found an open night.

* * *

It wasn't long before he wrote her a poem to express his affection for her.

He entitled it, "The Daisy."

The Daisy

One of the first things that attracted me,
Among the many that could be listed,
Was a small white daisy, painted by her eye
As if Mother Nature had kissed it.

It was small and dainty, kind of cute,
Not ostentatious at all,
But something more of an ornament,
Like that of a Christmas ball.
It wasn't the flower, cute as it was,
That made her so attractive to me,
It was her eyes, those beautiful eyes
That looked so affectionately.

They're just as beautiful as when we met,
The daisy attracting my view,
Whenever I look into those eyes
I can't help but say, I love you.

CHAPTER

3

□ □ □

"The question of life is not, How much time have we?
for in each day each of us has the same amount:
we have 'all there is.'
The question is, What shall we do with it?"
ANNA R. LINDSAY

NATHAN AND NATALIE DATED through their college
years, and when they were seniors, the subject of marriage seemed to come up again and again. It wasn't that
Nathan had proposed to her yet, it was just that they
occasionally discussed the possibility of marriage. To
be accurate, it was Natalie who would bring it up. She
was much more anxious than Nathan to make marriage
plans, since he seemed to be far more preoccupied with
plans for graduate school and a career. Whenever she
brought up the subject of marriage, he would switch

Michael K. Parson

the conversation and discuss his plans for going to law school.

"You do love me, don't you?" Natalie would ask.

"Of course I do! You know I do," Nathan insisted.

"Then why the reluctance to discuss getting married? I get the impression that it's not a priority for you. Don't you want to marry me?" she asked as her eyes began to tear up.

"Sweetheart," he said as he took both of her hands, "I love you, and I do want to marry you."

"Then why don't you want to make marriage plans? I'm supposing it's because you haven't actually proposed to me and don't want to jump the gun!"

"No, no, that's not it. While it's obviously true I haven't proposed, that doesn't mean I'm not planning on it." Her eyes opened wider when he said that.

Nathan continued, "Because it's all a matter of timing. If I'm going to be a good provider, I need to be successful in school. Then we can marry, settle down, and start a family without the burden and stress of school hanging over our heads," he explained.

"I understand, sweetie, but I don't see why we can't do both," she told him.

"Because I've seen how married students struggle to do both," he said to her. "And I feel I could concentrate more and be a better student without the burden of marriage."

"*Burden!* Is that what you think I'd be to you—a burden?"

Seeing her expression, he quickly responded, holding her close. "No, sweetheart, that's not what I meant." He kissed her then added, "I want to be able to show you all the love I have for you and not be distracted by so much schoolwork! Does that make sense?" he added.

"Yes, I guess it does. It's just that sometimes I feel I'm not the priority that I should be in our relationship."

"Oh, sweetheart, of course you are," he said, kissing her. "You are my life's highest priority. In fact, we haven't talked about it before, but once we're married, and if our first baby is a girl, I think we should name her 'Emily.'"

Natalie laughed and hugged him in agreement.

* * *

When Emily saw Natalie the next day, she could see that something seemed to be bothering her. "Natalie, is something wrong?"

"Oh, I don't know," Natalie responded.

"Well, I can tell that there's something troubling you. Come and sit down."

As Natalie pulled her chair out, she said, "It's just that Nathan is set on going to law school, and that's three more years of schooling!"

"Natalie, a lot of students go on to grad schools," Emily told her.

"Yes, but a lot of them get married first. Only he doesn't want to right now!"

"Have you tried talking to him about it?"

"Yes, but I think he's too stubborn and set in his ways, and I don't get the impression that he's going to change any time soon!" Natalie exclaimed as she began to cry.

Emily stayed with her for as long as she could, trying to console her. "Natalie, I guess you and Nathan will have to work this out. I don't know what else to tell you."

"Thanks for sitting with me, Emily. You're a good friend," Natalie told her as they hugged. "Oh, I forgot to mention," Natalie added, "Nathan said if our first baby is a girl, he wants to name her Emily!" They both laughed.

"Well," Emily added, "doesn't that show how important you are to him? He's already planning on the name of your baby!" They both laughed again.

* * *

Nathan had applied to several law schools, but Natalie had hoped he would attend Oklahoma State University because of its location in Norman, Oklahoma— only a couple of hours south of Stillwater. That would mean they would be able to see each other on weekends.

But she was again disappointed when he told her, "Sweetheart, I've decided to move to California to attend The University of Southern California in Los Angeles."

"What? I can't believe you would do this to me — to us!" Then she said in a tone of exasperation, "We could have seen each other every weekend! What were you thinking?"

When she protested, he explained, "But Natalie, they offered me the best financial aid package. I just couldn't pass it up. Please trust me on this."

Since Natalie was well aware that law school was going to be a serious financial struggle, she did not feel she could argue the point further. Also, she'd always felt that Nathan had a desire to get away from his hometown and feared that this was part of his motivation.

"Don't worry, Natalie," he told her. "In spite of the distance, we'll be able to stay close through phone calls, letters, and e-mails, and I promise I'll come home during breaks. It'll work out — you'll see."

She held him close and kissed him through her tears. "You promise?"

"Of course. I love you, sweetheart!" he said as he kissed her with much passion.

* * *

A family celebration was held in Nathan's honor before he left for Los Angeles. After the dinner, Nathan noticed Natalie was sitting by herself in the corner of the room. He excused himself, went to sit beside her, and put his arm around her.

"What's the matter, sweetheart?" he asked warmly.

"I just can't believe you are actually leaving tomorrow," she said with tears in her eyes.

He hugged her tightly and said, "I know just how you feel, because I feel exactly the same. Do you want to go for a drive so we can say our goodbyes more appropriately?" he asked with a knowing smile.

She smiled back. "Yes, I would love that."

Nathan told his family, "Natalie and I are going to go out for a little fresh air."

His uncle responded, "Oh, sure you are. The air in here isn't fresh enough for you, huh?"

They just smiled and kept walking out the door, while Nathan's mother reminded him that he needed to be up early for his flight. Then she asked, "Are you finished packing for the trip and ready to go in the morning?"

"Yes, Mom, I am." Then he added, "Well, almost!" His mother was about to say something more, but they had already closed the door.

They drove to a nearby park where they had often gone for picnics in the summer. He took her hand, and they walked to the top of a hill where they could have a view of the city. This was their favorite spot for watching sunsets in the evening.

As they scanned the horizon, Natalie asked him, "How long do you think it will be before the sun actually sets?"

"Probably within the hour," he responded. They talked about things related to their relationship and especially what they might do when they saw each other again. She then asked him, "How long do you think it will be before we'll see each other again?"

"I'm sure we'll both feel it will be too long! Once I'm there and can see my schedule, I'll be able to tell you more accurately."

"I hope you're right," she said as she hugged and kissed him again.

"Oh, look, the sun is starting to go down," he said, pointing to the western horizon.

She glanced a moment, commenting on the beauty of the sunset, but then quickly returned to kissing him.

After some time, Nathan looked at his watch and commented on the fact that they had ended up staying out much too late. As soon as he had made that comment, he noticed that his cell phone was ringing. It was his mother, but he did not answer. As they were leaving, he turned on the radio and they both laughed when they heard Ricky Nelson sing, *"It's late, it's late, we gotta get on home!"*

Nathan commented, "We'd better get going before my mother calls again!"

As would be expected, they had great difficulty saying goodbye to each other. While walking her to her door, he reminded her, "Now remember, sweetheart, how much I love you, and that I won't forget you." They stopped and he looked her in the eyes and declared, "I could never forget you. You are, and always will be, the love of my life!"

"You'd better not forget me," she told him. She then kissed him and declared, "I will always love you too!"

"And I promise to keep in touch," he said before one last hug and several last kisses. As he was walking to his car, he could hear her crying, so he hurried back for one more long hug and kiss. He then said, "When you are feeling lonely, just remember the poem I wrote for you. It will put a smile on your face!" He then added, "See, just like that!" And he jumped into his car and left with a honk and an extended wave out the window.

* * *

When Nathan arrived in Los Angeles, he was able to rent a small but comfortable bachelor apartment north of the law school on 30th Street. Even though it was small, it seemed perfect since he would be spending most of his waking hours in class or in the library. The apartment was a relatively short walk to campus, with the law school on the north side of Exposition Boulevard. He enjoyed what he called his daily "constitutionals" back and forth. It was good exercise, usually good weather, and a beautiful campus to walk through.

* * *

Nathan had underestimated how difficult law school would be, although it should not have been a surprise, since he was determined to be at the top of his class. In order to do so, he found he had to study nearly every free moment. Unfortunately, that meant he would have no time for relaxation in the evening, no weekend outings, and most importantly, no time for trips home to be with Natalie.

On the upcoming weekend, USC would be playing Oklahoma State in football. Nathan's schedule was so tight he did not plan to go to the game. However, his friends convinced him that he needed a break and should go with them to the Coliseum to watch the game. While they waited for the game to start, his friends asked him, "So, who do you plan to root for — USC or Oklahoma?" Since he would feel some loyalty to both schools, he thought for a moment and then said, "I'm going to cheer every time either team scores!"

* * *

All his hard work paid off by the end of his first year, and he qualified for the USC Law Review as well as a position on the Moot Court team. He excitedly called Natalie. "Hi sweetheart! I thought you should know that your future husband just qualified for the USC Law Review!"

Natalie, not fully understanding the significance, said, "Wow, congratulations! But what does that mean?"

He explained that because he had worked so hard, he not only made Law Review but won a position on the Moot Court team as well. "I wanted to do both, but they informed me that even though I qualified for both, I would have to decide between the two. So, I chose Law Review."

"What's Law Review?" she asked, still a little confused.

"I decided I wanted to become the kind of lawyer who could gain the respect that Atticus Finch did. Remember? We talked about him from the book and movie, *To Kill a Mockingbird*. And I figured that even though the Moot Court team would give me good experience, Law Review — which is a professional legal journal edited and published by the top students — would look better on future resumes and give me more respect."

After discussing more of his law school experiences, he said, "Well, I'd better get back to my studies. I don't want to get behind. I love you, sweetheart. I'll try to call you again this weekend."

"You'd better. I love you and miss you," she said before hanging up.

* * *

More Law School Experiences:

Professor Johnson was one of Nathan's favorite professors in law school. He seemed to take a special interest in Nathan and helped him get through some of his first-year struggles. On the first day of class, the professor walked in, set his books down on the table in front of the class, and announced, "The most important questions in life are where you came from, why you are here, and where you are going." He then went on to relate these questions to their law school experience and future careers.

Nathan got along well with Professor Johnson and often spent time with him in his office—not because of any problems, but because they just got along well together.

Another of Nathan's favorites was Professor Ron Garret. Nathan similarly spent time with him in his office. He was well aware that Professor Garret was popular with his students. During one of his visits, Nathan noticed an attractive plaque on the wall. It was an award recognizing outstanding teaching. What particularly impressed Nathan was that the award was not from the University but from one of the campus student organizations.

After reading the plaque, he commented to Professor Garret how impressive it was to be recognized by a student organization—The Latter-day Saint Student Association. He seemed quite pleased to have received it.

* * *

At the end of his first year of law school, Nathan sent the following note sharing another interesting experience with Natalie:

Hi Sweetheart,

I thought you would enjoy the following experience that happened in our Torts class this past week. It was the last day of class, just before finals started.

We were all tense and concerned about the final exam. There was a particular student—not known for academic excellence but well-known for expressing frustration with the class. He rode his Harley Davidson, dressed in his black leather jacket and pants, through the halls of the Gould

School of Law and into the classroom. He gunned his bike as much as he could on the top level of the classroom. I can't remember if he left right after that or stayed for the exam and then exited. The Professor did seem to acknowledge it with a smile.

Hope you enjoyed this!

Love and miss you,

Nathan

* * *

When his first-year final exams were over, he called Natalie. At first it was just small talk to avoid the most important news. Natalie finally asked him, "So, when will you be coming home?"

"Well, about that..." he hesitated.

"What do you mean? What now?" she asked with some confusion and emotion in her voice.

"That's why I called. A great opportunity has come up, and I'd be foolish not to accept it."

"Why do I get the feeling I'm not going to be excited about this?" she asked him.

"I'm sorry. Let me explain. I've been offered a very important opportunity— actually, more like a once in a lifetime opportunity," he clarified. "It's the chance to be a summer associate for a judge." There was only silence from Natalie, so he continued. "Very few students get invited to do this," he added.

When Nathan informed her that this would mean he would not be coming home for the summer, she protested, "But Nathan, we only saw each other for a short time at Christmas. I was really looking forward to this summer with you," she said with much more emotion.

"And I was too, Sweetie, but don't you see what an opportunity this is? I talked to two of my professors about it. One of them had done the same thing when he was in law school and strongly advised me to accept it. The other one was aware of the process of selection and said that I was the number one pick. And the judge I would be working with is under consideration for a Supreme Court nomination! He thought I'd be foolish not to accept it."

"I understand, but what about us?" she pleaded.

"Oh, Sweetheart, we'll have the rest of our lives together. But this will give me such an edge for the future. I just don't see how I could pass it up."

Michael K. Parson

"But what about our future? I feel like you're passing IT up!"

"Natalie, you know I'm doing all of this for you and for us."

"Are you? Sometimes I wonder."

Throughout the summer, Nathan called often and sent cards and notes to Natalie, realizing how difficult this was for her. He wanted to continually reassure her how important and helpful this was going to be for their future. He also emphasized how much he loved her and was looking forward to seeing her when he had a brief break at the end of the summer.

* * *

While Nathan was gone, Natalie spent time with and had many conversations with her best friend, Emily. Natalie told her how frustrated she was feeling with Nathan being away for so long.

"I think you need to get out more and socialize. You're spending too much time at home feeling lonely," Emily told her.

"I know, I know, but I still love Nathan and want to be loyal to him."

"I understand, but that doesn't mean you can't get out and meet people. I'm taking you out this weekend, and I won't take no for an answer!" She looked Natalie in the eyes waiting for a response.

After staring for over a minute, Natalie finally said, "Ok, I'll go."

Emily hugged her and said, "This will be great! We're going to have fun— you'll see."

Two days later Emily called Natalie and said, "Hey, Girl! How about we start with dinner at my house? My cousin Charlie will be here, and we'll be celebrating his master's degree. Then we can go out. How does that sound?"

Natalie hesitantly said, "I guess so. As long as you're not trying to set me up with your cousin!"

"Of course not! He's a great guy, but we'll just have dinner and then leave. No strings attached and no pressure, OK?"

"OK, I guess it will be fine."

When Natalie arrived on Friday evening, she was introduced to Emily's cousin, Charles McFarley. After shaking hands and a few pleasantries, Emily's mother spoke up. "Would you girls give me a hand in putting the food on the table?"

Michael K. Parson

Emily answered, "Sure, Mom — be right there."

Before they left the kitchen, Natalie stopped Emily and whispered in her ear, "He is *so* cute!"

Emily responded, "Oh, do you think so?"

They all sat down to a lovely dinner and enjoyed pleasant conversation. Charlie asked, "Natalie, how did you and Emily get together?"

"Well, actually," she began shyly, "we've known each other since grade school."

"Really? Then how come I've never met you before? Has Emily been keeping you hidden all these years?" he teased.

While Natalie was noticeably blushing, Emily came to her rescue. "No, of course not, Charlie. You just haven't been around very much! If you had, you would know Natalie. She's my best friend."

By the time dinner was over, Natalie noticed that nothing had been said about Nathan! Not by anyone, which was a relief to Natalie, who realized that she had not mentioned him either.

Emily's mother asked, "So, what have you girls got planned for the rest of the evening?"

"We thought we'd go to Eskimo Joes for a while, just to see who's there," Emily responded.

Charlie spoke up, "Oh, I love that place! It's a lot of fun," showing a personal interest.

Emily's mother asked, "You girls wouldn't mind if Charlie went along, would you?"

Emily looked at Natalie as if to ask her opinion, and more importantly, her permission. Natalie awkwardly paused, then said, "Sure, that would be fine."

The two girls sat in the front seat and Charlie in the back. When they arrived, Charlie jumped out, opened Natalie's door, and offered her his hand. She smiled, took his hand, and looked over at Emily, who just smiled.

After they had given their order to the waiter, Charlie excused himself to use the restroom. Emily quickly leaned toward Natalie and asked, "Well, how do you like Charlie?"

"Are you sure this is not a setup?" Natalie answered.

"No, I swear it's not," Emily quickly defended. "But still, how do you like him?"

"Well, you already know that I think he's really cute and very nice."

"And?" pressed Emily.

"What you probably want to know is, if I wasn't practically engaged to Nathan, yes, I guess I'd be interested."

Emily, seeing that Charlie was coming back, just smiled and said nothing.

When they returned to Emily's house, Natalie said she needed to return home. She thanked Emily's mother for the dinner and as she was about to leave, Charlie said, "It was very nice to meet you, Natalie. Let me walk you to your car."

"Oh, no, that's alright. I'll be fine," Natalie said to him.

"Now, what kind of a gentleman would I be if I let you walk to your car in the dark by yourself? You never know what kind of evil characters might be lurking outside, just waiting for a cute, innocent girl to come outside all alone," he told her with a teasing grin. When he saw her smile at him, he said, "Now, I won't take no for an answer." He took her by the arm and began walking her out.

When Natalie entered her home, the phone was ringing. She picked it up and immediately recognized Emily's voice.

"OK friend, you owe me a report on how things went with Charlie. What did he say?" she wanted to know.

"He asked me out!" Natalie told her.

"What? Oh my gosh! What did you say?"

"I didn't know what to say," she admitted.

"Well, you must have said something!"

"He said there was a very important event at his school where he would be honored, and he wanted some company. He said he couldn't imagine better company, and would I please go with him."

"When I told him I was dating someone, he said, 'That's ok,' and that he promised to be a perfect gentleman."

"So, again, what did you say?" Emily asked with a bit of impatience.

After a long pause, Natalie admitted, "I said 'yes'!"

"Okay, Natalie, do you promise you will call me after your date with him to tell me how it went?"

"Sure."

"You promise?"

"Yes, I promise," she said as she giggled.

When Natalie called Emily after the date, Emily asked her, "So, was he a perfect gentleman?" and she giggled when she asked.

"Yes, I'd say so."

"Well, what did he do?" Emily wanted to know.

"He did hold my hand as we walked in and out of the building."

"And?" Emily pressed her, "Did he kiss you?" she wanted to know.

Michael K. Parson

Natalie paused for several seconds until Emily asked, "Natalie, he kissed you, didn't he?"

Natalie finally said, "Well, just on the cheek."

"Oh, what did you do?"

"Well, nothing. I just smiled and said goodnight."

* * *

Within a few weeks Natalie wrote Nathan the following letter:

Dear Nathan,

I'm sure you are doing well in your job with the judge and that this will be a great opportunity for "your" future. I love you and want you to be happy in whatever your plans will be. But, Nathan, I can't help but feel that I may not be a part of that future. For some time now I have not felt that I am the most important thing in your life. You need to decide what you really want. As for me, I have decided I want and need more in a relationship. While you are deciding what really is most important to you, I think we should be free to date others. When you have made up your mind, I hope we will not have drifted too far apart. I wish you only the best and much happiness in whatever you decide.

Love, Natalie.

After reading her letter, Nathan was somewhat confused and then a little upset. *Doesn't she understand how much I'm sacrificing for her?* He tried to put it out of his mind for the present and concentrate on the research he was doing for the judge. Later that night, while trying to sleep, he could not get Natalie's letter out of his mind. He felt bad and said to himself, "Of course she's the most important thing in my life. I just never imagined how overwhelming this job with the judge would be."

When he had time, he responded to her, without mentioning her suggestion that they be free to date others. *Easy for her to say,* he thought, *she has the time and luxury to date, but that's simply a luxury I don't have!* However, he didn't want to sound bitter or negative, so to avoid driving a wedge between them, he wrote:

Dear Natalie,

I understand how you feel, Sweetheart, and I don't blame you. The fault is mine. You know I love you, Natalie, and I promise that things will eventually get better. I will call you soon.

Love, Nathan.

Michael K. Parson

He did call her a week later when he had finished the project he was working on, and he sent her notes occasionally when he had time.

* * *

Shortly before the end of the fall semester of his second year, he received a card in the mail. He thought, *would this be an early Christmas card*? When he opened it, he read an announcement that Natalie was getting married the following April:

Mr. and Mrs. Henry Bremmer announce
the marriage of their daughter,
Natalie, to Charles McFarley.
To be married on April 5
in the Stillwater, Lutheran Church,
Stillwater, Oklahoma.
Please RSVP.

This was quite a shock to Nathan. *I guess I was so wrapped up in what I was doing, I just didn't see this coming*, he thought. *And I guess it's pretty obvious that she's been dating!*

For a day or so, whenever he thought about it, he noticed that he felt a dizzy spell coming on, and even felt nauseated on occasion. He got very little sleep because he couldn't stop thinking about the fact that he had just lost the love of his life!

At first, he thought about calling her to try to talk her out of it, but he realized it was his fault. *She's moved on, and I don't blame her. I would have gone home for Christmas, but now it would be too awkward. Perhaps, in a way, I've moved on, too.* He finally decided to close out this chapter of their life together with a note.

Dear Natalie,

I received your wedding announcement this week. Congratulations. Please know that I sincerely wish you all the happiness in the world. You deserve it. I am sure your future husband is a wonderful person. He is definitely a lucky man. I hope you will be able to forgive me for the disappointment I have caused you. You really do deserve better. Best wishes to you always.

Love, Nathan

P.S. I still promise that I will never forget you!

When Natalie received Nathan's letter, she cried. She had anticipated that he would probably be shocked and disappointed by her announcement, but she had really expected a different reaction. *Why didn't he argue and fight for me?* she wondered. *I thought he really loved me. Now I'm not so sure.* And she wiped her eyes.

* * *

He would have liked to have gone home at the end of the summer, just to be home again and maybe to see Natalie again. But he knew it was over between them, so he decided not to. He used the excuse that Law Review students were encouraged to come back early, and he wanted to get an early start on his first edit of the new semester.

* * *

Nathan had not dated at all before Natalie's wedding announcement. He wanted to be loyal to her, but mostly, he admitted, he was too busy. During his third year, he did attend a party with friends but did not stay long. In addition to being too busy, Nathan went through a bit of a depression due to Natalie's upcoming wedding.

He thought, *The best thing in my life is now lost. It's not fair! You do everything you can to prepare a good future for yourself and the person you love, and the universe works against you!*

I have serious doubts whether I'll ever have another relationship like Natalie!

It took him a while, but he was finally able to focus on his studies and put thoughts of Natalie behind him.

* * *

During his last semester, Nathan excitedly looked forward to his graduation. His parents had hoped to attend his commencement in early May, but Nathan's mother had been developing Alzheimer's for many months. His father was her main caretaker and the closer it got to the graduation, the more her health declined.

It was with much sadness that Nathan received his Juris Doctorate degree at the head of his class without his parents being there. He was confident that they were proud of him. His father had emphasized this in a phone call the day before he graduated.

Nathan had planned to make a trip home after graduation to visit his mother. His father warned him, "I can't promise that your mom will even recognize you, Son. Sometimes she doesn't even recognize me!" he exclaimed with a touch of humor.

"I understand, Dad. It sounds like she is slipping away fast. I just need to see her. I really miss her, and I fear I may not get another opportunity to see her again."

"All right, Son. It will be great to have you home again anyway."

"I'm looking forward to it, regardless of the circumstances," Nathan told him.

His father added, "Do you think you will want to visit Natalie, or would that be too awkward for you?"

Nathan thought for a moment. "Yeah, it would be. I wouldn't know what to say to her, other than 'Congratulations,' and I've already said that. If the wedding hadn't already occurred, well, that might have changed things. I'm OK with it now, though. Natalie is past history." Tears welled up in his eyes as he said those last words. He knew they were true, but it hurt so much to admit them.

His dad responded, "I understand. We're looking forward to your visit, as short as it may be."

"Thanks, Dad. Love you. See you soon."

Nathan enjoyed his visit home but had difficulty seeing his mother. When he first arrived, his dad walked in first and said, "Sweetheart, here's our son, Nathan."

As she looked up, she smiled and said, "Oh Nathan, it's so good to see you. Where have you been?"

"I've been away at law school in Los Angeles," he explained as he gave her a hug. But as he waited for a response, she seemed to be in another world.

Even though she was not able to communicate with him, he was still glad he came, although he wondered if he would even see her again in this life.

CHAPTER
4

◨ ◨ ◨

"We live in deeds, not years; in thoughts, not breaths;
in feelings, not in figures on a dial.
We should count time by heart-throbs.
He most lives who thinks most,
feels the noblest, acts the best."
PHILLIP JAMES BAILEY

Law Firm and Partnership

SINCE NATHAN HAD GRADUATED with honors, he was very optimistic about his professional future. It was not long before he was hired into a prestigious law firm in Los Angeles— Herkermer, Spemwalter, and McFarquarson. The three distinguished individuals, after whom the law office was named, had long since died. This was an old and established firm that was now led by the grandson and grand nephews of the founders.

He did all he could to be the best of all the new attorneys hired that year. All of the partners seemed impressed with his dedication and hard work. He made every effort to be one of the first ones in the office every morning and occasionally he was the one who turned out the lights at night.

It was well known that Nathan would always ask the partners if they had anything else they wanted him to do before they left the office. Not always, but sometimes, they would respond to his request, "Why yes, Nathan, I could use your help with this matter. Thanks for asking."

In order to get ahead more quickly, he volunteered to be in charge of the firm's annual picnic — the yearly "Clothing for the Homeless" drive. He did his best to avoid making it appear that he was being too aggressive in trying to get ahead, even though he really was. He hoped the partners would not see it that way. His goal was to ensure that in their eyes, he stood superior to the other attorneys.

* * *

Late in his second year with the firm, he decided he could afford to move to a bigger and nicer apartment downtown. He wanted to live much closer to the office so that he could be at work within minutes instead of over half an hour.

As Nathan began his third year with the firm, he began hearing rumors of "partnership," something which usually took several years. Two of the senior partners would be retiring within the year, and it had been decided to add three new ones to replace them. Based on the rumors, Nathan's name seemed to be under consideration. However, whenever his name was mentioned, he tried to pretend he either didn't hear it or acted as if it would never happen.

* * *

Nathan's firm strongly discouraged dating among the employees. It was not that it was forbidden, you just knew that if you wanted to get ahead, you avoided it, and Nathan was very aggressive in wanting to get ahead. Occasionally he felt that Anna, one of the secretaries, was being a little too friendly and flirtatious. She would always make it a point to say "hello" to him and find excuses to pass his desk so she could say something or at least smile at him. She would regularly bring him some kind of treat and leave it on his desk, and if he wasn't there for some reason, she would leave it with a note.

Whenever any of these things happened, he would always smile and thank her, but he purposely tried to avoid these flirtations. In fact, when he was informed that Anna had requested a transfer to become Nathan's secretary, he requested one of the older secretaries instead to make sure he was not tempted or distracted in realizing his career goals.

Nathan was quite flattered by all the attention he was receiving and under other circumstances might have responded positively to them. After all, Natalie was no longer in the picture, so he was free to date anyone. But since his heart was more into wanting to make partner, he wasn't about to let anything or anyone distract him from that goal.

Anna wasn't the only secretary interested in him. Some were naturally attracted to Nathan because they saw him as one of the more handsome attorneys. Then there were those who could see how ambitious he was and who recognized that he would be able to support them in a manner to which they would like to become accustomed.

On one occasion, while using the restroom, Nathan overheard his fellow attorneys talking about him. They did not know he was in one of the stalls. One of them said, "It doesn't matter whose toes he steps on while climbing the corporate ladder, as long as he climbs."

Another added, "Particularly if he climbs faster than everyone else." The others chuckled in agreement.

As he heard their comments he thought, *Well, I guess I know whom I can trust. This information will come in handy when I'm a full partner.*

* * *

One Friday morning when Nathan came to work, his secretary, Helen Johnston, informed him, "Mr. Spemwalter asked to see you as soon as you arrived in the office."

"Thank you, Helen," he said, fully understanding what this could mean. Mr. Spemwalter was the one who would make final partnership decisions. As he walked down the hall, he began wishing he had arrived in the office earlier. He was actually on time but felt that it never hurts to impress the boss even more.

As he arrived at the corner office, the secretary greeted him and said, "Just knock on the door."

Since he was always conscious of making a good impression, he quickly thought, *If I knock too timidly, he may see it as a sign of weakness, but if I knock too loudly, he might think I'm too forward or aggressive.* He took a deep breath and knocked three times—somewhere between "too soft" and "annoying," hoping to make the right impression.

The door opened quickly, and he was greeted with, "Nathan, come in and have a seat."

"Thank you, sir," Nathan responded, as he sat down across from him, adjusting the chair.

After a moment of pleasantries, Mr. Spemwalter said, "I'll get right to the point. Nathan, we've had our eye on you for some time now. All of the partners have been impressed with your dedication."

"Thank you, sir, that's quite a compliment," he responded.

"We were especially impressed with your handling of the lawsuit against the firm," Nathan was told.

"I was just trying to do my job, *sir.*"

"And we were very much gratified to see the settlement you negotiated. You saved the firm millions." Nathan was pleased to see the very large smile on Mr. Spemwalter's face.

"I'm honored that you were pleased, sir."

"We were more than pleased, Nathan. And it's for those reasons and many more that we are inviting you to be a partner at H.S.M." Nathan could hardly contain himself and hoped his smile was not too noticeable. "What do you have to say, young man?"

"Me, sir? But with all the attorneys we have here, I never imagined you would invite me."

"Nonsense, my boy. You stand head and shoulders above the others. You're just the caliber of young attorney we're looking for in a partner," he responded.

"Well, sir, if you feel that way, then yes, I'd be honored to accept." They shook hands warmly and chatted about what would be expected of a new partner.

As Nathan rose from his chair, Mr. Spemwalter walked around his desk and reminded him that his first partners' meeting would be at 8 a.m. the next Friday. "Now Nathan, you don't want to be late to your first partners' meeting, do you?" he asked facetiously, patting him on the back.

"No, sir, I'll be here before 8 o'clock," Nathan told him.

"I've noticed that about you—always punctual," he said as Nathan went out the door.

Mr. Spemwalter's secretary saw the smile on Nathan's face as he came out of the office. "Congratulations," she said while handing him a large envelope. "Now, you will need a complete physical."

"A physical?" he questioned.

"It's just a routine procedure," she explained.

Michael K. Parson

"But I'm pretty healthy. Is that really necessary?"

"Only if you want to be a partner," she laughed, patting him on the shoulder. "Your benefits package will significantly increase, so it's covered. Your appointment is already scheduled for Monday morning. It's all here in this envelope."

He thanked her and went back to his office. Nathan could hardly believe what had just happened. He wanted to scream, dance, and jump for joy! It wasn't long before the others being made partner stopped by his office to congratulate each other.

While they were all in this congratulatory mood, Nathan listened to their voices to see if he recognized any of them from the "restroom incident," but he did not. Before they left his office, he had already decided not to worry about it anymore. "Getting even" was no longer a priority to him. He would simply watch them over the next few months, study their character and probably do nothing.

That evening he called his dad who was quite excited for him. "Nathan, that's wonderful. Congratulations! I always knew you had it in you! Why don't you fly home this weekend for a little celebration?" his dad suggested. "You could fly home early Saturday morning and return Sunday evening." Relatives and a few close friends would be invited, he explained. "I don't suppose you'd want to invite Natalie, would you?" his dad asked jokingly.

"No, not really," Nathan responded. "I'll see you tomorrow."

After his arrival home, Nathan went to the store to pick up supplies for the party. On this Saturday afternoon, he was surprised and maybe a little shocked when he ran into Natalie at the market.

"Nathan, what are you doing back in town?"

"Oh, hi Natalie. I'm just in town for the weekend."

"Really, what's the occasion?" she asked with some surprise. "Your mother hasn't passed away already, has she?"

"No, no, nothing like that."

"Well, it must be something important to bring you all the way home!"

"It sort of is. I was made a partner at my law firm this week, and my dad wanted to celebrate with family and friends," he told her.

"Wow, congratulations!" she said, giving him a hug.

As he felt her embrace, it brought back memories of how often he had felt her affectionate touch. He had forgotten how much he had missed that feeling, but in that instant, it had all come back. He realized how much he wanted to hold her longer, but knew he could not, so he let go.

"Thanks, Natalie. I appreciate that," he said to her, smiling.

"It's too bad your mother isn't well enough to really enjoy this," she told him.

"Yeah, you're right. It's been great to see her but so sad that she hardly recognizes anyone. It was still worth coming home for, though. So, how's married life treating you?" he asked to quickly change the subject.

"Oh, it's wonderful! What about you? Are you dating anyone now?"

"No, not really. Things have been way too busy at work. In fact, the last date I had was with you!"

"Seriously? My gosh, you don't get out very much, do you?" They both laughed.

After an uncomfortable pause, Nathan said, "Well, I'd better get home with all of this. Dad will be wondering what happened to me. Great to see you, Natalie."

"You too, Nathan, and congratulations again," she told him with another quick hug that might have been interpreted as a little inappropriate, had it been seen by her husband.

As Nathan got into his car and drove off, he couldn't help but think of what might have been had he and Natalie married. He had to admit to himself that he still had feelings for her but quickly tried to put those thoughts out of his mind.

Nathan had no way of knowing how Natalie was really feeling. As she drove out of the parking lot, he did not see her wiping away the tears from her eyes. She tried not to but could not help remembering her wedding reception as she stood in the reception line greeting and hugging her guests. She did not think anyone noticed her glancing toward the door with hopeful thoughts of seeing Nathan enter.

After the reception, while Emily was saying her goodbyes, she commented to Natalie that she couldn't help but notice her looking back toward the door. She asked, "Were you looking for someone in particular?"

She noticed Natalie blushing as she said, "No, no one in particular."

"Could you have been looking for Nathan?" she asked.

Natalie did not respond for several seconds, then finally said, "I've always felt bad about how our relationship ended."

"You are happy with Charlie, though, are you not?" Emily inquired.

"Oh, yes, I'm very happy."

"So, was that just force of habit when you looked toward the door for Nathan? Or something else?"

"No, it had to be force of habit, because I really am very happy with Charlie!"

Emily gave her a look that could have meant she didn't believe her, but Natalie decided to ignore it, regardless of what it meant.

CHAPTER

5

□ □ □

Physical Exam and Results

ON MONDAY MORNING Nathan arrived early at the hospital. "Hi, I'm Nathan Reynolds. My firm made an appointment for a complete physical. Am I in the right place?" he asked the receptionist.

"Yes, you are. You need to fill out these forms before the doctor can see you."

Nathan looked at the stack of forms, then at his watch. "Are you sure he'll still have time to see me when I'm finished with all of these?"

She smiled, "Oh, yes. Your appointment isn't for another half hour."

After showing an expression of surprise, he said, "I was told to be here at 8 o'clock. Was that not correct?"

"Yes, that's correct, but your appointment with the doctor isn't until 8:30. You'll need that time to finish the forms," she said with a grin. "Good luck."

He was asked to fill out pages of information about his health history and if he had ever had certain symptoms and diseases, some of which he could not even pronounce. When the doctor reviewed the information, he asked Nathan about some of his responses.

"You say you've been experiencing headaches, nausea, and dizziness?"

"Yes, but I'm sure it's due to the stress I've been under these last few months. It's really nothing," he assured the doctor.

"You're probably right. I've found that the best doctor is often the patient himself. You know how you normally feel, and if there's been a lot of stress lately, then maybe you're right," the doctor told him with a reassuring look. "If there is anything else, the tests will tell us."

When the tests were completed, Nathan thought he had done well and felt confident he was healthy, so he did not concern himself with worrying about the results. He thanked the doctor and hurried back to his office where, as a new partner, he had a pile of cases to supervise.

* * *

Two days later, the receptionist called and asked Nathan to come in and meet with the doctor for the test results. He was preparing for a deposition on an important case and felt that this was just too much of an imposition. "Can't you just mail the results to me or just tell me over the phone?" he asked impatiently.

"Only the doctor can tell you the results," the receptionist replied and insisted that it was necessary for him to come in.

"Oh, that's just so you can charge me for another visit," came the rude reply.

"There is no charge for this follow-up appointment," she said very politely.

"All right, I'll be in tomorrow morning." He was frustrated about having to lose the morning hours but didn't worry any more about it because of the deposition.

The next morning, as he sat waiting for the doctor, he began feeling more stressed by the minute. He was irritated that he hadn't been seen yet. "Doesn't the doctor know that I have a life too?" he asked the receptionist.

"The doctor will be with you in just a moment," she responded.

Looking her in the eye, he said firmly, "Please remind the doctor that I am an attorney, and if he doesn't see me soon, I'm going to deduct my time from his bill. And if he thinks his hourly rate is high, wait till he sees mine!"

"I'm very sorry for any inconvenience, Mr. Reynolds. I'm sure it will be just another moment." Then, from the look on Nathan's face, she braced herself for another rude remark.

Just then, the door opened, and the doctor said, "Good morning, Nathan, thank you for coming in." After sitting down, the doctor asked, "Can I get you something?"

"No, no, just explain why I needed to come back in."

"Of course. I wanted to discuss your test results with you, and it was necessary to do so in person."

"Why couldn't you have just mailed them to me or told me over the phone? I know I'm in good shape," he insisted.

"Well, in many ways you are," the doctor agreed.

"What do you mean, 'in many ways'?"

"I now know why you've been experiencing head-aches, nausea, and dizziness."

"I already know the cause. I told you. I'm just stressed out because of the pressure at work!"

"Actually, the stress is not the cause, but it has probably aggravated your symptoms." The doctor then went over the test results. They talked for some time.

Nathan did not say much as he left the hospital. He went back to work but did not see anyone. Before closing his door, he asked his secretary, "Helen, would you please hold any calls? I would rather not be disturbed for any reason."

"Of course, Mr. Reynolds."

At about 2 p.m. he left the office without giving his secretary any explanation. Helen assumed he was just leaving for a late lunch.

He drove out to the beach, took off his coat, tie, and shoes, and rolled up his pants above the ankles so he could walk along the ocean. He seemed to be in another world as he walked and then sat on the beach. He could see no one within a hundred yards.

He stayed until the sun began to dip below the horizon. He had never seen the sun setting on the ocean before. But after seeing it for the first time, he realized what he had been missing.

He thought of the many times he and Natalie had walked along the shores of Lake Carl Blackwell in the evening and watched the sunset. These thoughts brought back memories of Natalie, and he wished she was there to comfort him.

As he walked along the beach, with the evening breeze blowing on him, he was reminded of a popular song he and Natalie had enjoyed listening to. He couldn't remember all the words, but some of them still touched him as he struggled to quietly sing a few of them, realizing that he wasn't doing justice to the original song.

The summer wind, came blowin' in,
It lingered there to touch your hair.
Two sweethearts, But then,
I lost you to the summer wind!

He used his shirtsleeves to wipe the tears from his eyes and returned to his car. While he was driving, it began to rain, and he could see lightning to the north in the foothills. Nathan had not seen this kind of a storm since moving from Oklahoma. By the time he arrived home, it was getting very late. He pulled into the underground parking lot of his new townhouse and entered his home.

He did not feel hungry, but more out of habit, he prepared something to eat. He just sat there, moving the food around his plate. He felt devastated by the diagnosis — inoperable brain tumor! And there was no question. The doctor had checked and double checked. "Perhaps as much as a year to live," he had been told— but with emphasis on the *perhaps*.

Later that night, he lay in his bed in the darkened room. He was staring out the window at the rain reflecting the light from the corner streetlamp. As he lay there, he wondered whether his life was even worth living anymore.

He felt guilty for thinking such thoughts, especially when he considered all the things he wanted to accomplish—all the plans he had made. Now he would never realize any of those dreams. He felt life was cheating him out of all he had worked for. It seemed he had been given a death sentence to be carried out in less than 12 months, and he was quickly sinking into despair. Again, he thought about Natalie and realized that, under the circumstances, perhaps it was better that the two of them had not married.

At that moment he found himself uttering a prayer. Nathan had not prayed since childhood, but now, feeling totally desperate and alone, he begged, "Oh please, someone please help me. I don't know where to turn."

He lay there for some time, weeping. As he sank deeper into depression, he began to have thoughts of suicide. He felt so desperate that he uttered, "Why shouldn't I take my life? The next 12 months — if that's how much I have — won't be worth living."

CHAPTER

6

□　□　□

The Messenger and the Maladic Transfer:

IT WAS SOME TIME BEFORE Nathan began to sense that he was no longer alone in the room. At first, fear began to overtake him as he looked to his left, then to the right.

He could hear and almost feel the pounding of a heart, and he instantly thought of Edgar Allan Poe's story "The Tell-Tale Heart," where the murderer had buried his victim beneath the floorboards.

In the story, he began to hear what he first thought was the heartbeat of his victim. But then he realized it was his own heart that was pounding in his chest. In those few seconds, Nathan thought of every horror story or movie he had ever read, seen, or heard of. But, like the story, Nathan realized that it was his own heart that he heard and felt beating!

The feeling and fear were so strong that he finally fumbled with the lamp on his nightstand and turned on the light but saw no one. Being able to see the entire room, he began to feel more calm. Yet, still fearing that someone was there with him, he called out, "Who's there?"

He heard nothing but could not shake the feeling that he was not alone. As he continued to search the room, he reached under his bed for a baseball bat he kept there for security — in case he needed to defend himself. He had heard of a burglary in his building and bought the bat for protection. Again, raising his voice, he demanded, "Who's there?"

To his utter shock, he heard, "I'm here."

He quickly scanned the entire room but still saw nothing. "Where?" he asked, thinking the person must be hiding.

When Nathan again heard the voice, "I'm right here," it was not loud or sharp but a very soft voice. To his amazement, when he heard the voice this time, he was not frightened but felt perfectly calm and peaceful.

"I'm here, right next to you," the voice said.

Nathan looked slightly to the right where he had already scanned several times, and there he was. Standing only a few feet away was the kindest looking gentleman he had ever seen. At first Nathan was speechless, but the man seemed so harmless and loving that he finally asked, "Are you God?"

The gentleman smiled and seemed genuinely amused. "No, Nathaniel, I'm not God."

"You know my name?" Nathan asked, surprised.

"Of course, I do," the stranger replied.

"I don't feel that you are here to do me any harm."

"Oh, no, just the opposite," the stranger insisted.

"Who are you then? Are you my guardian angel?"

"No, not really." Again, he seemed amused.

"Is this the first time you've come to me?" Nathan wanted to know.

"No, there have been other times."

"Have you always been with me?"

"No, not always."

Nathan noticed that the stranger no longer seemed amused. He was genuinely interested in his questions

Michael K. Parson

and sensed Nathan felt impatiently anxious, wanting to know more but only getting short, simple answers to his questions. "Well, when have you come before?"

"Remember the time when you were a boy, and you went hiking with your best friend in the canyon?"

"Yes, I remember. I was with Tommy Layton."

"That's right, and Tommy slipped and fell off the edge and was hanging on?" the stranger reminded him.

"Yes. I didn't know what to do because Tommy was a lot heavier than I was, and I couldn't pull him up."

"And do you remember what happened next?"

He was surprised how well he remembered everything — as if it had just happened. He had no idea the stranger was helping him to remember. "Tommy couldn't hold on any longer." Nathan got emotional as he relived the experience. His voice stuttered as he tried to explain what had happened. "I knew if I didn't pull him up right then, Tommy would drop to his death."

"And what happened? What did you do?" the stranger asked.

"I'm not sure. Somehow, I got the strength to pull him up, even though I had already tried and failed," he said while wiping his eyes.

The stranger smiled, as if proud of Nathan. "That was a great day, wasn't it?"

He looked at the stranger as if he had discovered a great secret and asked, "Was that you?"

"No, Nathaniel, that was you."

"What do you mean? How was it me?"

"I was there all right, but it was *you* who did it."

"Wait a minute," Nathan quickly responded. "It just came back to me. I remember that just before I pulled Tommy up, I heard a voice—a very strong and commanding voice—say, 'PULL HIM UP, NOW!' Was that you?"

The stranger smiled and said, "Yes, Nathaniel, that was me. A second later and it would have been too late. That commanding voice gave you the strength to do what had to be done."

"Wow, I remember it all so clearly now. How different our lives would have been had you not helped me that day. I'm so grateful, thank you." The stranger just smiled at him.

Nathan instantly remembered one of his high school years when his PE class was getting ready to choose up sides to play baseball. Before they had started, Tommy said to Nathan, "You won't be picked!"

Nathan answered, "Why not?"

"Because, as you know, you're not very good!" Tommy responded.

Nathan thought, *He's right, I'm usually picked last!*

Nathan then recalled his grandfather telling him to "win your enemies over with kindness."

He then told Tommy, "If I was selecting the team, I'd pick *you* first!" He could tell that he must have said the right thing by the way Tommy smiled at him. And from then on, they were the best of friends.

"So, who are you then?" he asked the stranger.

"I'm a messenger."

"A messenger?" Nathan asked as the stranger nodded, smiling. "So, what's your message?"

"That is something you will have to figure out. But I am here to help you."

"Help me? Help me do what?"

"Didn't you say you needed help?"

"No, I didn't say that."

"Are you sure? Because I distinctly heard you ask for help."

Nathan couldn't believe what he was hearing and wondered, *Could this possibly be the answer to my prayer?*

The messenger responded, "Yes."

"Yes, what?" Nathan asked.

"Yes, I not only could be, but *I am* the answer to your prayer," the messenger said.

"How did you know what I was thinking?"

The stranger just smiled and said, "How would you like me to help you?"

As shocked as he still was, Nathan felt he could trust him. *After all he seems to be able to read my thoughts.* "Why has this happened to me?" he asked.

"Why has what happened to you?" the messenger replied.

"You've got to know why I'm so depressed. I don't deserve to have this disease."

"Deserve?" the messenger asked, questioning Nathan's choice of words. "Do you think this is some kind of punishment?"

"Well, maybe. It feels like it."

"So, you think everyone who gets sick or injured is being punished for something?"

Nathan thought for a second. *It does seem that way sometimes. Couldn't God do that?*

"Whether He could or would do that are two different questions."

Nathan stared at him, not fully comprehending. "But I was raised to believe that if I was bad, God would punish me."

"Too often you might think you're being punished for something, when in reality, it's the natural consequences of your choices and decisions. You are here to make choices. Life is a test to see if you are willing to make good and wise choices or bad and poor choices. It's a test. If you were punished for every bad thing you did, most people would make good choices just to avoid being punished and not because they want to be good."

"So, my cancer is the consequence of my bad choices?"

"Illness, whether the common cold or terminal cancer, is part of mortal life. Just because a person is seriously ill does not mean God is punishing them for something they did or didn't do."

"So, you can't do anything about my cancer, then?"

"What is it you want me to do about it?"

"I don't know, can't you take it away? You know, like a miracle!"

"Is that what you had in mind when you prayed for help?"

"I don't know. I'm so confused. I wish I could just give it away, just give it to someone else." Nathan thought for a moment. "Yes, why not? Is that possible? It should be."

"Is what possible?" the messenger responded.

"Giving or transferring my cancer to someone else?"

"To whom would you transfer it?"

"I don't know. You must understand these things better than I do."

"Are you suggesting a 'maladic transfer'?"

"A what?" Nathan asked, getting completely confused.

"A maladic transfer. Isn't that what you're asking for? Transferring your malady to someone else?"

"Are you sure there is such a thing in the English language?" he questioned hesitantly.

"Never mind that. It is what you're asking for, isn't it?"

"Well, yes, I guess so. Is that possible?"

"Many things are possible."

"Really? But how would it work? I mean, this really would be some kind of a miracle, wouldn't it? Do you just take it away and give it to someone else?"

Staring at him, the messenger asked, "Have you considered the consequences of what you're asking?"

Michael K. Parson

"What consequences? I get rid of it and someone else gets it!"

"And you think that's fair?" the messenger replied.

"Fair! Where was the fairness when I got it in the first place? Or was my cancer transferred to me from someone else?"

"Do you think it's as easy as that to get rid of? Have you considered that maybe you're supposed to have this malady, and the other person isn't?"

"What do you mean?" Nathan responded.

"Maybe there are lessons you need to learn that can only come through this kind of experience."

"Then find someone else who needs the lessons more than I do!" Nathan insisted.

After a long pause, the messenger looked him in the eyes. "I think you may have something there."

"What's that supposed to mean?" he asked, even more confused.

"You think that if there is someone more 'deserving' than you, then your cancer should be transferred to them. Is that right?"

"Yes, I guess so, but you would know men's hearts and minds better than I would. I think..."

"That's it!"

"What? What's it?" Nathan asked.

"Your mission will be to find someone who is more deserving."

"My mission?" he exclaimed.

"Yes, your mission. Remember, I'm just the messenger," he said smiling.

"Well, how will I know if they're more deserving?"

"It must be someone who could learn or grow more from your experience than you could."

"And when I find this person?"

"*If* you find this person, we'll talk about it."

At that instant Nathan was distracted by the sound of thunder and a flash of lightning. He glanced quickly out the window and back again. As he looked back, the messenger was gone, and all was quiet.

Nathan just sat there, totally confused and even dumbfounded! He wondered just what he was supposed to do or even to think.

Michael K. Parson

CHAPTER

7

□ □ □

"Does not health mean harmony? A healthy body is good; but a soul in right health, —it is the thing beyond all others to be prayed for; the blessedest thing this earth receives of Heaven."

THOMAS CARLYLE

NATHAN WOKE UP LATE the next morning. When he looked at the time, he quickly jumped out of bed and dressed. He then skipped breakfast and rushed off to work. He realized he was behind schedule for the partners' meeting and was angry with himself for being late for this first one.

As he rushed into the office, the secretary greeted him. "Good morning, Mr. Reynolds. They're waiting for you."

"How long ago did they start?" he asked without missing a stride.

"Just a few minutes is all. You haven't missed much."

He was mentally kicking himself, realizing he had missed an opportunity to make an important impression at his first partners' meeting. He quietly slipped in, hoping to sit near the door. His heart sank as Mr. Spemwalter spoke up.

"Nathan, come and sit here," he said, motioning to the only empty seat in the room, which happened to be next to his. "We were worried about you. Did you have any difficulty?"

"Uh, yes sir, I did," he answered with a quivering voice.

"Nothing serious I hope?" Mr. Spemwalter continued to question.

"No, sir, everything's fine now." After sitting down, he was afraid to look around, sure everyone was watching him. He appreciated Mr. Spemwalter not making too big of a deal about his tardiness, but the message was clear. Nathan firmly believed that perception is everything, and he had just lost the chance to impress the rest of the partners. He wondered what the other new partners were thinking.

After the meeting, Nathan was about to go to his office when Mr. Spemwalter's secretary asked him, "How was your visit with the doctor?" He stopped, and his eyes widened. He had completely forgotten about it in the rush and excitement of the meeting. Her question brought to his mind the realization of the diagnosis. He felt in that moment as if his whole world had come crashing in on him. "Are you all right, sir? You look white as a sheet," she told him.

Shocked and depressed, he quickly excused himself and went into the bathroom and rinsed off his face. As he looked at himself in the mirror, he remembered the messenger and for a moment could not tell if it was a dream or reality. Since he knew the diagnosis was real, he hoped the messenger was real also. If so, he felt that what the messenger had said was his only hope.

Later in the afternoon, he had a meeting with another attorney with whom he had become friends. His name was Mortimer Bertram. Growing up, he had always been teased about his name, but since beginning law school it was worse. "Morty, have you ever heard of a 'maladic transfer'?" he asked him.

"A what?" he responded.

"Ma-la-dic trans-fer," he enunciated.

"What's that?" he questioned, looking quite confused.

Nathan felt embarrassed as he realized how ridiculous his question must have sounded and wished he had not asked it. "Never mind, just something I dreamt about."

Too embarrassed and confused to remain in the office, he left early and began driving. Within minutes, his cell phone rang, but he decided to ignore it. However, too curious not to at least see who was calling, he noticed it was his doctor. Pulling over, he called him back.

"Nathan, I wanted to discuss possible treatments to slow down the cancer and hopefully buy you more time."

"I don't think so, doctor. I have an alternative treatment I want to try first."

"Nathan, I would warn you about alternative treatments. Most just give false hope. Why don't you come in and we can talk about it?"

"I don't think so," he said again. "At least, not at this time."

"But Nathan, that's what I'm concerned about — time. You won't have much of it left."

After saying goodbye, he continued driving but wasn't sure where he was going. He only knew he did not want to be at work or go home. He found himself returning to the beach, to the same location he had been the night before. He felt drawn to it, again walking along the water without paying any attention to the time. He again sat in the sand waiting for the sunset, still without any concept of time.

As he pondered whether the experience he had the night before was real or not, he had an overpowering feeling come over him. It was something he did not remember feeling before. He thought of it as a peaceful feeling, kind of a calming influence that seemed to remove all doubt. He felt the experience was a bit overwhelming. He just knew it was real but wondered how and why he was so sure. He remembered and reflected on an experience he had as a boy.

His parents used to take him to church. On a particular Sunday, the minister was preaching about faith. Nathan couldn't remember much of what he said but did recall that he said something like, "Faith is more than a belief — it's an assurance." He wondered why he remembered that. All he knew was he had an "assurance" that the experience he had with the messenger was real. Based on this assurance, Nathan determined to proceed with confidence in finding a likely candidate for the maladic transfer.

As the sun finally set on the horizon, he decided to go home. As he traveled, he couldn't get his mind off of the events of the last 24 hours. He ate a little and prepared for bed. While in bed, he pondered a great deal regarding the stranger's message of the night before and gratefully fell asleep.

CHAPTER

8

Michael K. Parson

▣   ▣   ▣

There is an eternity behind and an eternity before,
and this little speck in the center, however long, is
but comparatively a minute.
JOHN BROWN

THE NEXT MORNING, Nathan thought long and hard
about who would be a suitable candidate. He sat in
the upstairs window of his townhouse, looking out on
the street. He watched every person who passed and
wondered. He quickly decided that he did not want to
transfer his malady to anyone he knew. *That would be
awkward*, he thought.

Each stranger who passed was a possibility. He grew
tired of the process until he spotted someone from the
neighborhood. He was a teenager, about fifteen years
old. Nathan did not know much about him — just that
his name was Rubio. From what the neighbors had told

him, Rubio seemed to always be hanging around and getting into trouble. He often picked on the younger kids, stole things from the market, and was disrespectful to everyone.

Nathan's car stereo had been stolen a month before. He had no proof but strongly suspected Rubio. As he watched him, Nathan began talking to himself. "It looks to me like he's looking for trouble. Why don't his parents discipline that kid? He never seems to be in school. Whenever I see him, he looks suspicious. Wait, what's he doing behind my car?" Nathan had moved his car from the underground parking lot to the street so he could leave more quickly for work.

He saw Rubio picking the lock to his trunk. Nathan ran down the stairs and outside, but by the time he got there, Rubio was gone — but not empty handed. "That thief stole my new CD player!" he said after looking into his empty trunk. He went inside and picked up the phone to call the police. While it was ringing, he quickly hung up. A thought had just occurred to him. *Rubio! Yes, he's perfect!*

He smiled as he sat down and thought about his choice for the maladic transfer. *That kid's a juvenile delinquent. It will serve him right.*

Once he was sure about Rubio, he wondered what should happen next. *The messenger said that when I found the right person, we'd talk about it. Well, I've found him. How long do I have to wait?*

He quickly got dressed and went to work. Throughout the day he was sure he had made the right choice.

When he returned home, he went for a walk in the park near his townhouse. As he sat on a bench, thinking, he watched the children playing. There was a child, about three years old, with someone Nathan assumed was his grandfather. The child had fallen, and the grandfather quickly went to his aid. "Here, let me help you," he said.

Nathan remembered an incident with his own grandfather. He thought, *I have not thought of it since it happened over twenty years ago. I was walking with my grandfather to go to the park. We had to cross the street, but I was afraid. My grandfather said to me, "Don't be afraid. Take my hand and I'll help you."* Nathan smiled at the memory.

Thinking about the incident caused him to reflect upon another experience that happened when he was in the fifth grade. *I had a friend named John. I remember going over to his house and asking his mother if John could play. She told me that John was very sick, but she let* him come to the door to say "hello." I did not know at the time how sick he was but later found out it was cancer. A short time later I heard that John had died. I remember wishing I had done more for him—been more of a friend to him. His experience must have been frightening. Maybe I could have helped, in some small way made it easier. Nathan reflected.

Now, after seeing the child in the park and thinking about his friend in fifth grade, Nathan was having second thoughts. Maybe giving my cancer to a kid isn't such a good idea. Even if he is a juvenile delinquent!

CHAPTER
9

Michael K. Parson

□ □ □

Life can only be understood backwards;
but it must be lived forwards.
SOREN KIERKEGAARD

Early in December, Nathan began noticing a homeless man at the freeway off- ramp where he exited to get to work. He held a sign in his hand that read "Homeless. Please help. God bless you."

His first thought was that the man was merely taking advantage of people, so he ignored him. After seeing him for several more days, he wondered why anyone would subject themselves to such humiliation. Out of curiosity, more than anything, he finally decided to stop and talk to him. Nathan discovered that the man really was homeless, and he lived on a street in the Skid Row neighborhood of downtown Los Angeles. His name was Nick.

Michael K. Parson

That evening, Nathan couldn't get the man out of his mind. He thought, *If he's homeless, then he couldn't have much of a life to look forward to, so it really won't make any difference anyway. And when he's gone, there won't be anyone who will miss him. He's perfect.*

Ever since he had his experience with Rubio, Nathan realized he needed to take more time and not rush into a decision. He wanted to be absolutely sure in choosing a candidate. A few days later, during his lunch hour, Nathan went for a walk in Downtown Los Angeles. He found himself walking near Skid Row, where he saw a man who appeared to be homeless, sitting on the sidewalk. He approached him. "Hi, how's it going?" he said as he approached.

"How's what going?" the man said abruptly.

"I just wondered how you were doing, that's all."

"Why? Are you with the government?"

"No, no, I'm doing research on the homeless in Los Angeles. I just wanted to talk to you."

"A reporter, are ya?"

"Yes, could we talk?"

"What did ya wanna know?"

"First of all, I'm interested in knowing how you live here on the streets."

"Not very well," the man said with a slight chuckle.

Nathan smiled. "Could you tell me how you live from day to day? Where you sleep, eat, go to the bathroom, etc?"

"Gettin' kinda personal, aren't ya?"

"I didn't mean to sound rude or too personal. I'd just like to know."

"It's hard for the well-to-do to know what it's like. We often sleep on the streets, in an alley, and sometimes on park benches. When it's cold we try to find a bed in one of the shelters, if we're lucky. If not, any kind of shelter will do. Sometimes even a cardboard box."

"What about food?"

"Sometimes we get to eat at the mission down the street. And then sometimes it might be out of a dumpster."

"A dumpster?" Nathan asked with surprise.

"Sure, especially behind a restaurant or a market. You'd be surprised how much food gets thrown away!"

"So, you do that every day?"

"Not every day. We often beg for food. If anybody gives us money, we might buy something." Nathan nodded to indicate he understood, then waited, hoping he would continue.

Michael K. Parson

"And as far as a bathroom, well, whatever we can find. I always hope for a public restroom, otherwise, it may be the bushes. Whichever comes first," he grinned, revealing his lack of dental care. Nathan made a mental note to check with USC's dental school to see if they have a dental outreach program and if anything could be done for him.

Nathan asked, "Do you, by any chance, know a man by the name of Nick? He's often at the freeway off-ramp at Hoover and West 20th Street."

The man interrupted, "Ya mean St. Nick? Sure, everybody knows St. Nick."

"Why do you call him St. Nick?" Nathan asked.

"Because he's always giving us stuff or doing things for all of us. He helps everybody."

"What do you mean? Like share the money he collects?"

"Yeah, if ya need it. If ya need food, he'll help. If one of us is sick, he's there to help. He's like Santa Claus — St. Nick!"

"Anything else you gained or learned from Nick?"

"Well, yeah. Nick taught us how to survive on the street and showed us where we could always find a warm place to sleep."

"Where's that?" Nathan asked with interest.

"A hospital ER can be a good last resort. If you complain about a stomach ache, you'll end up spending the night waiting to be seen."

"What if they call you in to see the doctor?" Nathan asked.

"First of all, they probably won't. But if they do, then you either get a free doctor's appointment, or you just tell them you're feeling better now!"

Nathan just raised his eyebrows and showed an expression of surprise. "Sounds like you've done that before."

"Yes, more times than I'd like to remember."

"Another good place to crash is a hotel conference room."

"Really, why?"

"Because they're never used at night, and they're comfortable. Although, some hotels lock them up at night."

"What if they catch you?"

"If you don't look homeless, when security finds you, just pretend you are drunk and wandered in by accident and fell asleep."

"Have you done that?"

Michael K. Parson

"Yes, several times."

"And were you ever caught?"

"Sure, about half the time."

"What about homeless shelters?" Nathan asked.

"They're great if you can get in. The worse the weather is, the harder it is to get into one. The secret is getting in as early as possible! Once, when I had cleaned up really good and had decent clothes on, I spent the night at the Metropolitan Opera."

"Really, how did you manage that?" Nathan could hardly believe that but wanted to understand.

"I showed up just as everyone was coming out. I used the restroom, lingered awhile, then slipped into the ladies' room."

"Why the ladies' room?" Nathan asked.

"Because it has a separate powder room-complete with comfy couches. I turned the lights out and made myself at home."

"And no one came in to check on you?" Nathan wanted to know.

"Yeah, someone opened the door, but since the light was out and the room was quiet, I was left to sleep for the night and with a bathroom in the next room," he chuckled.

Nathan was not so sure anymore about making the transfer. He thanked the man, gave him some money, and moved on down the street. He noticed several other homeless men come out of an old storefront church. It was some kind of a mission where people from the street were fed. As he entered, he got a few stares from those who were leaving. Some were still eating, and others were just sitting around tables talking, playing checkers, or other games.

He looked around the walls. There were newspaper articles about the mission and its history. He saw pictures of the mayor, other dignitaries, and even famous movie stars and sports heroes serving food to the homeless over the holidays.

The item on the wall that intrigued him the most was a framed poem entitled "The Beggar." Nathan carefully read:

One day as I went along my way,
And while traveling, I passed a man.
His clothes were rags, his shoes all worn,
And he carried a sign in his hand.

I thought, "Now, what in the world does he want?
Why doesn't he go get a job?

How does a man get as low as he has?
What if his intent is to rob?"

I pass him daily, as I travel along,
And hope that our eyes never meet.
I really want nothing to do with the man,
So I cross to the side of the street.

I have sometimes thought, "Why not help him
And share with him part of my day?
Why make the poor man beg vainly
And continue to turn him away?"

Perhaps I might say, "I won't help him
Why should I give of myself?
The man's fate is just, it's really his fault,
He has brought it upon himself

Then I realize, "Are we not all beggars,

To God, we all play a part.
It isn't the outward appearance He sees,
But inside, He looks at the heart."

My friend, the beggar, seems different somehow,
And I remember that someone has said,
When we serve others, whether beggar or friend,
It is God we are serving instead."

After reading the poem, Nathan began to see the homeless, and particularly Nick, in a very different light. The words of the poem caused him to think, *Even if I don't think he has much of a life, and he doesn't have any family, there are a lot of people here who will not only miss him but will suffer a loss if he's not around.*

* * *

As Nathan was walking back to work, he noticed a young boy, maybe eight years of age, on the street. He was only wearing a thin shirt and appeared to be freezing. Los Angeles, usually known for mild weather in the wintertime, was having an unusual cold spell.

Nathan asked him, "What are you doing out in this weather? Aren't you cold?"

"Yeah, but what am I supposed to do?" the boy responded.

"Don't you have a warm coat to wear?"

"No. I did have one, but I grew out of it. It's too small. My little brother wears it now."

"So, what's your name, kid?" he asked him.

"It's Jacob."

"Why doesn't your mother buy you a new one, Jacob?"

"She can't afford it. She said Santa might bring me one."

"That's still a few weeks away. What will you do until then?"

"I just try to stay warm. I usually run home from school when it's really cold. I hope Santa brings me one like yours."

Nathan was wearing a beautiful leather jacket. He looked at his jacket and then at Jacob and said, "You like this one, huh?"

"Yeah, it's cool. Where did you get it?"

He thought back to an earlier Christmas at home when his mother gave it to him and said, "You may not need this in Los Angeles, but Merry Christmas anyway."

Nathan responded to the boy, "Actually, it was a Christmas present."

"From Santa?" the boy asked, his eyes growing wider.

Nathan nodded and smiled, then took off the jacket and said, "Let's just see what size you wear."

When Jacob put it on, he said, "Wow, what a cool jacket — and really warm, too!"

"It is a cool looking jacket, but it's even warmer to wear. Looks a little big on you though, don't you think?"

"No, it's perfect. This is the size I hope Santa brings, 'cause then I could wear it longer before I grow out of it. Do you think Santa still has any of these?" Jacob asked.

Nathan ruffled the boy's hair. "Merry Christmas Jacob," he said, and began to walk away.

"Hey mister! You forgot your jacket!" Jacob called.

"No, I didn't. Merry Christmas."

"Hey, who are you? Are you Santa?"

Nathan, who was several steps away, turned and said, "No, I'm not Santa. But I'm helping him today."

Jacob's eyes widened more, "Thanks mister, and tell Santa thanks, too."

Nathan smiled and waved, then turned the corner out of sight.

* * *

When he returned to work, he saw Mr. Spemwalter in the hall and told him he had some great ideas for the annual "Clothing for the Homeless Day."

"Sounds good. Come in and let's talk about it."

He shared with him his experience and asked what he knew about USC's Dental Outreach Program. He was encouraged to go to the dental school to see what he could find out. Before leaving, Mr. Spemwalter called him back. "Let me share a story with you. Please keep it confidential, but you need to know about it." He told Nathan about a homeless man that he had met years before.

"This fellow was really trying to better himself. He happened to know a woman who was a maid at a local hotel. He had saved her from a very dangerous situation, and she wanted to repay his kindness. She knew he lived on the streets, so she would let him into an empty room after the guest had checked out. He would sleep, shower, and get dressed. As soon as he left, she would clean the room. To repay her, he went out each day, looking for employment. I hired him as a custodian until he eventually got back on his feet."

Nathan was amazed and very touched. He said, "That experience reminds me of a homeless man that I just met."

Later, as he sat at his desk, he wondered what he would do now. He realized that, after his experience downtown, he could not transfer his malady to the homeless man, Nick, nor to any homeless person.

CHAPTER
10

Michael K. Parson

◻ ◻ ◻

"As if you could kill time
without injuring eternity!"
HENRY DAVID THOREAU

AFTER TWO ATTEMPTS AND FAILURES, Nathan was again having second thoughts about transferring his cancer to someone else but was still willing to go through with it. To add to his problems, his health was progressively getting worse, and he was beginning to feel desperate.

He contacted his doctor and inquired as to what medication he could take to at least slow down the process in order to give him the little more time the doctor had previously talked about, at least until he could find the right candidate. The doctor did write him a prescription, hoping it might be of some help, but also urged Nathan to come into his office so he could do more for him.

* * *

One evening, while Nathan prepared his dinner, he heard a portion of a news story on television. Something about a man who was convicted of murder and his sentence was the death penalty. One of the people being interviewed commented, "He doesn't deserve to live for what he did!" That comment caused Nathan to think, *If he doesn't deserve to live, why wouldn't he be the perfect candidate for the maladic transfer?*

Nathan hurried out to buy a newspaper. He wanted to get as much information as possible. He read about a liquor store robbery where a two-bit hoodlum, named Buddy Jenkins, had stolen some beer and demanded that the man behind the counter empty the cash register drawer into a bag and give it to him. He pointed a gun at him and said, "Hurry, or I'll blow your brains out!" The employee did so, but as soon as he handed the bag to Buddy, he pushed the alarm button. Buddy had already made his way out the door, but when he heard the alarm, he turned back and shot the employee in the face, killing him instantly.

There was another employee in the back who saw the whole thing and testified at Jenkin's trial. He was convicted of first-degree murder and sentenced to die in the gas chamber.

The article went on to explain that even though he was sentenced to death, with all the appeals he would likely get, it will take years for him to pay the ultimate price for his crime.

Nathan thought about it off and on throughout the evening, and then it occurred to him — *Wait a minute. If he's going to be put to death in prison, then why wouldn't he be the perfect candidate for the maladic transfer? I'd actually be doing him a favor because he'd be dying of natural causes!*

After reading the article a second time he felt sure that his search was finally over. "Buddy Jenkins is the man," he said over and over.

"It almost seems too good to be true, but I've got to be absolutely sure," he said, looking at himself in the mirror. With that, he decided he wanted to meet Buddy in person. He drove to the State Penitentiary in Victorville, California to see the man who "doesn't deserve to live."

During his travel, he could not help thinking of Buddy Jenkins. As he arrived, he said to himself, "He's got to be

Michael K. Parson

the man! He's perfect. If he's not, then I don't know what else I'll do. I can't imagine a more perfect candidate! My problem is that I'm running out of time." Nathan was sure he was running out of time because his headaches had been increasing regularly.

When he arrived at the prison, he asked permission to see the prisoner, Buddy Jenkins. The guard on duty asked to see some ID. When Nathan showed his ID proving that he was an attorney he was told, "Yes, you can see him, but right now his mother is with him. You can go up to the reception area, and after his mother leaves, you can see him — if the prisoner is willing."

While Nathan was waiting, he could see the prisoner talking to his mother. He had expected to see a rough looking, hardened criminal but was quite surprised to see a young man who had a rather innocent looking face.

What surprised Nathan the most was how remorseful he looked. There were no reporters nor photographers present for him to play the repentant prisoner role. Here he was, alone with his mother, begging her to forgive him for what he had done — both for the murder and for disappointing her so much. They were both in tears.

Nathan overheard him tell his mother through his tears how much he had changed. "Mama, I'm so sorry for my crimes. I'd give anything if I hadn't killed that man — anything! I wish with all my heart that I could have another chance to prove that I can still be a good person. Please forgive me mama."

Nathan was touched by the man's contrition and felt sorry for him and for what he had done to his mother. Buddy Jenkins was not even aware that Nathan was observing him, but in this brief encounter, he felt compassion for him and for his mother, causing him to change his mind.

Actually, it wasn't just his mind that was changing. Nathan was becoming aware of a much greater change within himself!

* * *

While Nathan walked back to his car, he came upon a woman about to exit her vehicle. She was well dressed, and her driver had not gotten out of the car yet. Nathan could not help noticing that she reminded him of Buddy Jenkin's mother, whom he had just left. "May I help you?" he asked, offering her his hand.

"No, young man, I'm okay. I can get out of my car by myself, thank you. I'm not as old or helpless as you might think," she answered back, with a tone of sarcasm.

Not wanting to offend her, but anxious that she understand his intent, he said, "It's not a matter of age or strength. You're a lady! It's a matter of honor and respect." He again offered his hand, with a bit of a smile, not sure what she would do.

The woman hesitated but then smiled back and took his hand. As he assisted her out of her car, she commented, "There are not many knights in shining armor anymore! I guess the days of chivalry are not dead after all! Thank you, young man," she said, and they smiled at each other.

CHAPTER

11

Michael K. Parson

□ □ □

"If you live up to your privileges the angels
cannot be restrained from being your associates"
JOSEPH SMITH

WITHIN A MATTER OF WEEKS, Nathan lay in his bed with a splitting headache. He suddenly felt the presence of someone else in his room. He raised his head from his pillow and turned to see that the messenger had come to see him again. Nathan no longer thought of him as a stranger and was genuinely glad to see him. As he sat up in bed and started to greet him, his visitor asked, "So, what have you decided?"

"What, no 'Hello, how are you?'" Nathan asked him.

"Hello, Nathaniel, and I already know how you are. So, what have you decided?"

"I've decided to keep my own malady."

Michael K. Parson

"Why is that?" the messenger wanted to know, showing sincere compassion.

"But you already know, don't you?"

"I still want to hear it from you."

Nathan sighed then said, "Because I'm tired of trying to play God."

"And what do you mean by that?"

"I don't want to be the judge of whether someone should live or die. I picked three different people that I thought at the time were perfect. They seemed so deserving. But they all had good reasons to live, so I just couldn't give it to them."

"And *you* didn't have good reasons to live?"

"I suppose when facing death, you can always think of good reasons to live."

"What about finding someone who could learn more from your experience than you could?" the messenger asked.

"I now believe that everyone has to learn from their own experiences. And I realize I've learned so much more about myself than I probably could have learned without this experience."

The messenger just smiled and seemed genuinely pleased. But Nathan could tell that he was about to leave again. "Wait, can't you stay? I have so many things to ask you."

"Remember, I'm just a messenger."

"But you never told me your message," Nathan quickly responded.

The messenger smiled and answered, "You've already figured it out."

"What do you mean? I don't remember figuring anything out."

"You just said it better than I could."

Nathan had such a sad look on his face that the messenger asked him, "So, what's the problem?"

"I feel like such a failure," Nathan muttered.

"Why is that?" the messenger asked.

"Because I've made so many mistakes," he responded. I worry about the way I've treated people so many times. It's like I keep stumbling and falling down."

"Why do you consider those experiences failures?"

"Because I keep making the same mistakes!"

"Perhaps your 'failure' is failing to realize that not all of these experiences are failures but successes in going through experiences that make you grow and progress."

Nathan stared at the messenger and began to realize that he was becoming his mentor. He wasn't sure how

Michael K. Parson

to respond to such a new and profound thought. He instantly thought of several examples of seeming failures and what was gained.

He was surprised that he should think of these all of a sudden.

After bringing these examples to Nathan's memory, the messenger asked, "When you were a child, were you a failure just because you kept making mistakes — like falling down?"

"No, of course not."

"Why not? What's the difference?"

"Because I was only a child. I was just learning."

They both looked at each other, and the messenger began to smile. Nathan had become accustomed to that smile. "Okay, you're the messenger. What's your message now?"

"I would ask the same question. 'What's the difference?' You are a child of God. Aren't you still learning from your experiences? And does God consider you a failure because you sometimes repeat the same mistakes — like falling down?"

Nathan was gaining a new understanding but could again perceive that his new mentor was about to leave. "Well, can't we talk about it some more?"

"We'll have lots of time to talk," was the messenger's reply.

"When?" Nathan anxiously wanted to know.

"Very soon."

And with that he was gone. Nathan missed him already. Even with only these few brief encounters, he felt very close to this messenger, although he realized he didn't even know his name.

CHAPTER
12

Michael K. Parson

◻ ◻ ◻

Lives of great men all remind us
we can make our lives sublime,
and departing, leave behind us
footprints on the sands of time.
HENRY WADSWORTH LONGFELLOW

HE FELT TOO WEAK TO THINK or to worry about it anymore. The doctor had arranged for Nathan to be hospitalized for a few days, hoping they might be able to do something for him. When he was brought into his room, he was asked, "Nathan, do you want anything?"

"Just one thing," was his response.

"What's that? Something to eat or drink, or perhaps a movie?" the doctor suggested.

"No, nothing like that. Do you remember when I first came in for my physical and testing a year ago?"

"Yes, of course," the doctor replied.

Michael K. Parson

"Your receptionist then, is she still working with you?" He seemed anxious to know.

"Yes, Mary is still working with me. But you should know — she's married."

Nathan smiled. "It's not what you think. Could she come in to see me? I just need to tell her something."

"She's working now. I'll see that she comes up before she goes to lunch."

"Thank you. It's very important," Nathan replied with a very serious look on his face.

"No problem. I'll make sure you see her."

A little after noon, Mary entered his room. "Did you want to see me, Mr. Reynolds?"

"Yes, thank you for coming, I appreciate it very much. Please, sit down," he said, pointing to the chair next to his bed.

"Thank you. Are they making you comfortable here?" she asked.

"Yes, as best they can under the circumstances. I guess you know how little time they are giving me."

"Oh, Mr. Reynolds, I'm so sorry. Can I do anything for you — anything at all?"

"You already have, just by being here."

"I don't understand, what do you mean?"

"Do you remember a year ago when we first met?"

"Yes, of course I do."

"Well, if you do, you will also remember how rude and unkind I was to you."

"Oh, Mr. Reynolds, you don't need to apologize for anything," she insisted.

"Oh, yes, I do. I don't want to leave without you knowing how sorry I am. I should never have spoken to you the way I did."

He was so contrite and genuinely sorry it brought tears to her eyes. "Mr. Reynolds, I..."

"Please, call me Nathan."

She smiled, "Alright, Nathan, of course I accept your apology, but I hardly remember the incident. I forgive you and thank you for being so considerate in wanting me to know you are sorry. Please don't let it bother you anymore."

"Thank you, you're very kind. I wish I was as kind as you a year ago," he responded.

"Thank you. Now you're being very kind. Are you sure there isn't anything I can do for you?"

"No, you've done more than enough by coming to see me."

"Well then, I'm going to stop in to check on you again, just to see if there is anything you need or would like."

"Sure, that would be fine. I'll try and stick around long enough to see you again," he said smiling, and he heard her chuckle as she went out the door.

* * *

Three days later, while listening to the song "Over the Rainbow" on the radio, he remembered how his grandfather used to sing it to him when he was a young boy. And he remembered his grandfather's comment, "Sounds a little like heaven, doesn't it?" Nathan thought how the words did seem to describe his present condition. He seemed to remember one verse a little differently:

Somewhere over the rainbow
The dreams that you dream
Really do come true.

Nathan smiled at the words and wondered how long before they would be fulfilled for him. As he lay there thinking, he reached for his glass of water on the nightstand and took a drink. He then lay back on his pillow, thinking about the words from the song. Within a matter of seconds, he felt himself taking a huge breath, not realizing it would be his last, and quietly passed away.

He momentarily didn't even realize what had happened. He briefly struggled for a moment to get his breath and then found himself on the opposite side of the room. Everything seemed different. The room was the same, but he now saw it from a different perspective, and he noticed so many things he hadn't before.

He looked back at the bed and saw someone in it. He felt very puzzled, he couldn't understand why someone would be in his bed. When he looked closely, he was startled to discover that the person in the bed was himself. He wondered how that could be when he was actually on the other side of the room and not in bed! He thought, *I must be dreaming.* He tried to wake himself but couldn't.

He noticed a nurse peek into his room. He called to her to come and check on him, but she seemed to completely ignore him. She came back into his room a few moments later and placed an envelope on his nightstand and left the room. He wondered what it could be. He did notice the return address as his father's home address in Stillwater, Oklahoma and wanted to open it. Then the realization came to him — *I must be dead! Is this what death feels like?* The thought momentarily frightened him, when all of a sudden, he heard that voice that he had come to recognize.

"Don't be afraid. Take my hand and I'll help you."

Nathan turned and looked at him and grinned widely. "Grandpa! It was you all the time!" Nathan embraced him, wondering why he hadn't recognized him before. Understanding was instantly communicated to him, and he realized that before, he was seeing with his mortal eyes. Now he saw his grandpa with his spiritual eyes and completely recognized him.

As they walked away together toward the light, he said before they left the room, "But I wanted to open my dad's letter."

His Grandpa responded, "You'll know very soon what it said."

"Grandpa?"

"Yes, Nathaniel."

"Can I ask you something?"

"Of course," he answered.

"There's no such thing as a 'Maladic Transfer' is there?"

"No, Nathaniel," he said smiling. "There isn't."

"Then why did you tell me there was?"

"I didn't. You were the one who suggested it. I didn't discourage you because I knew this was an opportunity for you to discover some things about yourself and develop compassion for others. You're not at all the person you were when I first came to see you after you had prayed."

"And that was the message you eventually planned to give me, wasn't it?"

His grandfather just smiled in acknowledgement.

"And what about my name? In my baby book you wrote, 'I hope when you think about your name, you will think of Nathaniel of old and emulate the character of him who had no guile.' Was there also a special message in that for me?"

"Well, what do you think?" his grandfather asked him.

"As I look back on my life, I suppose I had lots of guile! But as you just pointed out, I'm not at all the same person anymore."

"I think I perceived that from your brief discussion with Mary," he told Nathan. He smiled at Nathan as they both felt the warmth of the light that now enveloped them. "Are you ready to see someone special?" he asked Nathan.

"Who, God?"

"No, not yet. That will come in due time."

"Who then?"

"There are several of your loved ones waiting in the next room to greet you."

"My relatives?"

"You're about to understand the contents of your father's letter. Go through that door and find out."

Nathan instantly found himself in the next room and exclaimed, "Mom!"

After embracing her for a long time, his mother said to him, "It's wonderful to see you, son. I guess you didn't have time to read your dad's letter, telling you that I had passed away. He had tried to reach you by phone but couldn't."

Nathan responded, "No, but it doesn't matter because here you are!"

She then said, "Look here, Nathan, you never met my parents — your grandparents — but here they are." He turned and saw two beautiful people and also embraced them for a long time. He commented, "You look so much more beautiful than I remember from your pictures!"

He then saw his father's mother whom he had never met but remembered her from pictures of her and his grandpa. He said, "Grandma," and embraced her also.

Nathan was overjoyed to meet so many of his relatives for the first time. Everywhere he turned he was constantly meeting more family members. At one point he heard a familiar voice say, "Hi Nathan." As he turned to see who it was, he was greatly surprised to see his childhood friend, John, who had died of cancer. And of course, he hugged him for a long time, too.

These kinds of glorious reunions seem to go on and on and on. Nathan said to his grandfather, "This is wonderful, grandpa, does it ever end?"

"No, Nathaniel, it will never end!"

CHAPTER

13

□ □ □

"We can't fully appreciate joyful reunions later
Without tearful separations now.
The only way to take sorrow out of death
Is to take love out of life."
RUSSELL M. NELSON

THE FUNERAL—STILLWATER, OKLAHOMA

A few days after Nathan's passing, his father, along with relatives and lots of friends, met in the Stillwater Lutheran Church to celebrate Nathan's short life. Nathan, along with his grandfather, found themselves in the rear of the church, as if seated high above everyone else. Even though seated in the rear, Nathan could see and hear everything as if seated on the front row.

He recognized everyone there that he knew. Even Natalie was there. He saw many who were in tears throughout the service, but he especially noticed Natalie

Michael K. Parson

had great difficulty holding back the tears. He noticed her husband, Charlie, comforting her. Nathan smiled and was pleased that she had married well, and he sensed she was happy, even though she was sad on this occasion.

Besides family, others spoke at the service. Mr. Spemwalter even spoke and talked about what a good attorney Nathan had been. He shared how Nathan was the number one pick to become partner and spoke of how sad they were to learn of his cancer. "Nathan was the hardest working attorney in our firm. From the time he was hired until his passing, he served well. We will greatly miss him."

"Goodbye, Nathan," he added as he pressed a tissue to his eyes. Nathan smiled when he heard those kind words and was glad he had made such an impact during the short time he worked there.

Graveside Service:

He also saw his father weeping at the graveside service and turned to his grandfather with a look that seemed to be asking permission to do something. His grandfather smiled and seemed to nod "yes!"

Nathan then placed his hand on his dad's shoulder with as much pressure as he was allowed to give. His dad seemed to feel something on his shoulder and placed his hand on the same spot, and Nathan felt that his dad must have sensed he was there.

Nathan asked his grandfather if he had any idea how long before his dad would be joining Nathan and his mother. His grandfather responded, "All I'm allowed to tell you is that time is different here compared to mortality. When you do see him again, you will think it has been a very short time since you last saw him. So, don't worry about it. In fact, you will be so busy you will hardly give it much thought. Just enjoy it, and as you can already see, it will be wonderful."

Postmortal Instruction:

His grandpa could see that Nathan was having some difficulty in understanding this new realm of the afterlife. He then shared with him a new understanding of what he is now and would soon be going through. "Nathan, let me explain some things that I learned after I first arrived here."

"Great, because I'm trying to figure all of this out, and I'm looking forward to having a lot more of the answers, like you grandpa," Nathan responded.

His grandpa then explained, "If you could see things as they are, and as you shall see and understand them, the experience of death is so trifling that you shall turn around and look back upon it and think, now that you have passed through it, that this is the greatest advantage of your whole existence. For you have passed from a state of sorrow, grief, mourning, misery, pain, anguish and disappointment into a state of existence, where you can enjoy life to the fullest extent as far as that can be done without a body. You will soon feel and say, 'My spirit is set free, I thirst no more, I want to sleep no more, I hunger no more, I tire no more. Nothing like pain or weariness, and I am full of life.'"

When Nathan heard his grandpa's explanation of his new spiritual existence, he was filled with joyful anticipation. He looked at his grandpa, smiled, and said, "I'm beginning to feel some of that already."

"Wonderful, but don't worry, Nathan, you'll have lots of help from family and friends to assist you along the way. I promise that you'll adjust. Just take it a day at a time."

Life is real! Life is earnest!
And the grave is not its goal;
Dust thou art, to dust returnest,
Was not spoken of the soul.
HENRY WADSWORTH LONGFELLOW

Michael K. Parson

www.ingramcontent.com/pod-product-compliance
Lightning Source LLC
Chambersburg PA
CBHW050852180626
46814CB00007B/2736